# AFTERMATH

## (AFTER #3)

## E. DAVIES

Publisher's Note: This is a work of fiction. Names, characters, places, and incidents are a product of the author's imagination. Locales and public names are sometimes used for atmospheric purposes. Any resemblance to actual people, living or dead, or to businesses, companies, events, institutions, or locales is completely coincidental.

Aftermath / E. Davies. – 1st ed.
ISBN: 978-1-912245-08-6

# AFTERMATH

"Come for me, baby!"

Charles was still strung out from his climax, sweat beading around his temples. His toes curled into the bed as Rob's weight pressed him back into the mattress.

The heat between their bodies was enough to make him melt. Rob never went easy, and he liked that about him.

Rob's hips stuttered as he lost his rhythm and rolled his head back. His fingernails bit into Charles's hip, and Charles, still sensitive, twitched under the pricks of pain.

Rob bared his teeth as he gasped. "I'm gonna, Charles. I'm so close. Fuck. You're so good. Oh, I love you."

Charles's heart pounded. He pressed his lips together to stop the response: *don't love me... just fuck me.*

"Yes!" Rob was coming, judging from the irregular, shallow thrusts and the gasps for breath. Then he dropped onto Charles, his arms weakening and no longer supporting his weight above him.

They were crushed together, and Charles had to get away.

Rob caught his breath first. "Jesus. That was good."

From the look in his eye as he pushed himself up onto an elbow and rolled off Charles, he knew exactly what he'd said and he was waiting for Charles to acknowledge it first.

Charles wasn't going to go within a million miles of there. "Mm," he agreed. It *had* been good, up until that little slip.

He wasn't dumb enough to think it was the kind of *I love your tight little ass* comment guys threw out there in the heat of the moment. Last time they wound up in his bed, Rob had hinted at the same thing.

He wanted more. They always wanted more.

Charles pushed back the sigh of exhaustion as he rolled onto his side, then grabbed his shirt.

"You can stay if you want. I'm not kicking you out." Rob tried hard to sound like he didn't care either way, but his voice was tight.

Charles felt bad for a moment. Rob was a nice enough guy —he didn't dislike him. But from the beginning, their deal had been friends with benefits, and now Rob wanted something different. Leading him on would be cruel.

So Charles shook his head. "I better go." He stepped into his jeans and slid the zipper up before he glanced over at Rob.

Rob said nothing for a moment, his eyes skimming over Charles's body.

Charles took the compliment and smiled as he pulled his t-shirt on. Unconsciously, his hand skimmed down the inside of his own arm, and the ridged marks still criss-crossing the skin there.

Then, Rob's hand closed around Charles's side, and he pulled him down to the bed for a kiss on the lips. "Can I see you again soon?"

Charles let him have the kiss, but not his attention. He pulled back again, stepping back from the bed to push his feet into his sandals. "I'd better not promise anything." He tried to keep his tone warm as he offered an apologetic smile.

Rob took the hint and flopped back against the bed with a casual nod. He wasn't defending himself or explaining away the *love you* moment. He wasn't trying to brush it off as the heat of the moment. That was the most telling sign.

Fuck. Charles was going to miss the sex.

"Yeah. See you, then."

"Bye."

Charles was a block away before he took a full, deep breath, and his shoulders dropped.

"Fuck's sake," he muttered under his breath, squinting around at the street signs to orient himself as he strode back toward State Street. He hadn't driven over, so he'd catch the bus from there.

Charles was off today—nobody had hang-gliding sessions or lessons booked. He'd thought to take a solo flight, just for himself, but now he was sluggish in the cool November air. As cool as Santa Barbara got, anyway.

Maybe he needed to stop sleeping with anyone more than once. It was limiting, but surely it would be more effective than his current strategy of waiting until the other guy tried to get close, then cutting him loose.

Sooner or later, everyone wanted strings.

Or maybe he was the problem. His chest tightened uncomfortably as he quickened his pace toward State Street. There was no time to mope today. He had shit to do.

Truth burned through his veins and pricked shame into his cheeks.

## JACE

"So, this is it?" Jace stared at the small, heavyset man who had been his friend and guide in the world of divorce over the last four weeks.

The weight pressing on him was lifting, except the weight in his hand—the file folders. The finalized judgement.

"You're done," Mr. Rodriguez told him. He was an anxious man, always shifting from one foot to the other, always looking around as if expecting some stray line in the settlement to creep around a corner and ambush him. For once, though, he stood solid and smiled. "We just have to wait until the six month period is up, and it'll be automatic."

Relief washed through Jace, hot and bright, yet with a painful edge. It was the first gasp of fresh air after a fire, the stiffening of a hose underhand as the first blast of water rushed through.

"I'm... very grateful for everything you've done."

"Oh, it's my job. You've paid me well for it," Mr. Rodriguez told him with a light laugh. "Now you can rest easy knowing it's all over. But, word of advice, Jace? Take some time for yourself."

Jace blinked at him. Since the fatality, since the investigation opened, since being put on administrative leave and mandatory counselling, he'd taken enough damn time for himself.

Still, he appreciated the thought.

"Thank you, sir."

They shook hands, and Jace took a moment to look around the steps of the small, squat law office where Mr. Rodriguez practiced, close to the Santa Barbara courthouse.

A fresh breeze ruffled their hair and broke the moment. Mr. Rodriguez shivered and nodded to his car. "I'm off, then. I'll be in touch on your D-Day."

Jace smiled. He had Divorce Day on his calendar.

"Feel free to call on me if there's a need, or just to let me know how you're getting on."

Jace smiled and raised a hand as he headed to his own car. He had no doubt the man meant it; they'd bumped into one or two former clients while eating out together and ironing out the details of the settlement. Everyone chatted with him like an old friend.

It all seemed so stark. The house was his; that was a relief. And at least they'd had separate cars. Much of the furniture had been Mike's, though. The house would be half-empty by the end of the week. He was supposed to be home to supervise and make sure Mike didn't take more than was his, but... fuck it. He couldn't look the man in the eye again.

He hadn't been able to since that terrible conversation. Mike had owned what he'd done, but that didn't make much of a difference when what he'd done had been several men, and enough Tina and G to knock out a racehorse.

Again.

Jace pushed aside the bitterness. That was over now. All his cajoling and wheedling, his careful watch kept on Mike's hobbies and friends, had done nothing.

His perfectly-planned life—trophy husband by twenty-five, fire chief by thirty, early retirement and Alaskan vacations—had unravelled at the seams.

This was supposed to be a victory—a chapter in his life done, or hell, a whole damn book closed. But it felt hollow.

He was single and *not* ready to mingle. For him, three months wasn't enough time to forget even a broken dish. The casserole dish Mike shattered last Thanksgiving had taken him until the new year to forgive... in retrospect, Mike had claimed it was from nerves about being around his family, but it had probably been a withdrawal symptom. How could he forget or forgive the man he'd pledged to spend his life with?

It had been just four weeks since their agreement to divorce, but it had been brewing for months. Mike hadn't done a good job of hiding what was going on ever since the summer.

He counted it as three months, because August was when the relationship had entered... probation, for lack of a better word. But mid-October, just four weeks ago, had been the final nail in the coffin—one of his firefighters had told him, per his new boyfriend, that Mike had been up to his usual games. Breaking probation.

A sigh escaped Jace as he started his car. He didn't have work to distract him, and he wasn't going to linger around the house watching Mike and his friends take the furniture.

It was amicable, as far as divorces went. No mailed anonymous hate letters or used condoms, no barbs thrown at each other from opposite sides of the courtroom.

Mostly because Mike knew Jace inside and out. More than anyone, he knew an apology, an act of revenge, or a friendly comment would meet the same stony-faced response from Jace.

So he didn't bother to try. That one fact gave Jace a tiny sliver of respect for him. Negated by the facts of the situation, but more than he gave some men.

Jace didn't forgive broken vows.

Lost in his own thoughts, he barely noticed himself driving the short distance down State Street until he was almost at the pier. This time of year, at least he didn't have to struggle for parking.

He could use a walk to clear his head. Legal documents were a slog to get through, and Mr. Rodriguez had insisted on reviewing the decision with him. It was very straightforward, but his lawyer hadn't wanted there to be confusion about what Mike was coming to take.

The beach was quiet this time of November, coming up on Thanksgiving in just a couple weeks.

Fuck. Jace was gonna be alone for that. And for the holiday season, and probably months more. Nobody wanted to date a man who was waiting five months to be legally single, and he didn't want to date for even longer than that.

Worst of all was the pity, the sympathy from others. Yesterday, at the memorial for Hans... Well, he didn't want that bullshit. He'd gotten over the worst of it weeks ago. Now it was straightforward facts.

He planned to spend Thanksgiving by himself, or busy with friends, if he could get away with it. His family wasn't big on time together, anyway, so he could pull it off for this season. They'd probably assume he was ashamed and give him space this year.

Fun fact: Jace and Mike had walked the length of the pier holding hands for the first time three years ago.

His footsteps echoed against the boards as he headed down to the end, hands tucked firmly in the pockets of his trousers.

Fun fact: Jace was thirty-three. It was the dead zone

between the pretty young men in their twenties and the older, desperate singles in their forties who'd take him for his body alone.

The breeze whipped up a light froth against the wavelets that lapped on the Santa Barbara shore. A few rollerbladers were skating along the concrete path that stretched along the harbor, holding onto each other and laughing.

Fun fact: Jace had never let his facade crack, even a little, in public; at least, not since that first fight in the restaurant two years ago, a year after he'd been made chief, when he'd seen the threat that Mike posed to his perfectly-planned life.

He leaned heavily on the wooden railing, glad for the chill in the air that morning, and the silence that had fallen over the tourist traps down here. No gift shop employees to scrutinize him as he rested his forehead on his braced forearms and let the hot tears trickle from the corners of his eyes into his rolled-up shirt sleeves.

2

CHARLIE

"When are you bringing Justin to see me? You boys make each other happy."

"Soon, Dad." The lie rolled off Charles's tongue at the same time as his smooth, warm smile. Years of this had taken the sting out of the words, so long as he didn't stop to think about them for too long. "I have to get going. I have a two o'clock tandem."

"Still doing that, eh? Madness."

Charles gave a fond smile at his dad as he rose from his seat by his father's table in the cafeteria. "And I still tell you, you'd love it."

He doubted his father would ever get to now. Besides, there was every chance he wouldn't remember it even if he did. The last few years had blurred too much into one, and his dad could only remember a few things since he'd moved into the home.

Including the fact that he'd dumped Justin. He'd never bothered telling his dad why, too afraid that *that*, of all things, would stick in his mind and be his fresh reality until... well.

*That* was what Charles had to try not to think about for too long.

"Oh, bah." His father waved him off impatiently, but Charles leaned down to hug him around his shoulders before straightening up. His father looked up at him with surprise, as always. And no wonder—they hadn't been affectionate, really, when he grew up. Not distant, but they'd kept space.

Too late for that. Charles wished he'd hugged his dad more all those years ago.

"What's that for?"

"Love you, Dad. Thanks for everything."

As always, his father gruffly smiled back and patted his cheek. "Go on, before you miss your appointment."

"Yes, sir." Charles playfully saluted and strode out of the cafeteria of the care home.

If the nurses at the front desk—Jenny and Karen today—noticed the tears in his eyes as he headed for the visitor parking, they were polite enough to pretend not to, as usual.

"Have a great one," he told them on instinct on the way out, but he didn't stop long enough to hear a response. He needed to get outside.

The cumulus clouds were perfectly formed today. It was going to be beautiful out there.

Charles had a better job than he could ask for. Hang-gliding was a hobby many spent their life savings pursuing while working to support it. He got to do it full-time; he got to teach new learners, talk to entire classes about his passion sometimes, and help people do charity gliding. He'd made long-term friendships with the experts he competed against and shared time and beer with afterward.

Lately, his specialty had been accommodating disabled people who wanted to hang-glide. His motor-driven system meant people didn't have to run with the glider, and he'd been trying to reach out to blind people in the community. He'd taken a seminar on visual interpretation, and it was a lot more work than he'd anticipated, but the few people he'd told his idea to had absolutely loved it.

*This* was why he didn't date. He had so much opportunity to do worthwhile things when he wasn't wasting his time chasing or being chased by men. There was only one thing he wanted from them, and he didn't need it as often these days as he had when he was twenty and fresh to Santa Barbara.

Or when he'd met Justin.

He didn't let himself take any longer to think about it than that as he drove to the cliffs of his usual gliding spot. Setup was mindless by now, letting him think about his visit with his dad, and his last coffee date with Ash.

The guy was going to learn fast. Ash was still holding off, though, since his first flight would be to raise funds for a male suicide charity in mid-December. Ash probably didn't have enough confidence in himself, and a healthy fear of heights. But he was fascinated by the mechanics of the tow mechanism, as a mechanic-in-training. Maybe Charles could use that to sneakily get Ash to glide more after that charity day, if all went well. It would help build his confidence.

And Charles had to talk to Jenny about the entertainment schedule, find out what was on for his Dad over Thanksgiving. His mom had left to join the circus—literally—when he was ten, so he didn't have that side of the family to worry about.

But as the only child, Charles had to visit his dad every Thanksgiving. Sometimes his dad's brothers would stop by and see him, but it was his duty.

Once the glider was double-checked for flight safety, the winds measured—all things he could do in his sleep by now—Charles took a moment to himself to sit on the grass next to his glider, his hand on the wing.

Without this, he didn't know if he would have made it through the long years after Justin. He almost hadn't. He'd taken it out on himself, body and soul.

Things were better now. Charles had found a precarious balance over the last five or ten years. He didn't feel the need to carve his pain onto his body, but some days, hang-gliding still hit that same spot in him.

It provided the adrenaline rushes that kept him sane. He'd done a few other adventure sports—base jumping, rock climbing, downhill skiing—and he'd felt that same joy in putting his life quite literally on the line, but nothing compared to this.

Because after the rush, besides the numbers running through his brain (*wind northeast at fifteen, better make it to that ridge lift*), there was serenity, too.

To Charles, it was a quiet but deeply fulfilling joy to hang nearly motionless in the air, looking at the world from so far up he could hardly breathe. His chest was tight as he pushed himself to hands and knees, then strapped himself into the harness of his glider.

Yeah. He had an hour to himself before he had to land and set up the winch for the tandem. He'd foot-launch.

Charles turned to the cliff edge and let the heat of fear flush through his body as a smile broke across his face.

It was time to fly.

3

— — —

JACE

"No, no, no—"

Jace choked off the words, squeezed his eyes shut for a moment, and drew one slow breath. Then, he pushed himself away from the sink. He fumbled to turn the cold water tap off. He couldn't stop the shivers running through his body. A few splashes of hot water helped him remember himself.

He dried his hands and stared in the mirror, pushing his hair back. He needed a good shave, and he looked pale and shaky even to his own eyes.

Fucking dreams. They weren't constant, but they still struck out of the blue. At least once a week, he saw Hans disappearing into the flames. No matter what he did in those dreams, the result was always the same: Hans limp, splayed across the pavement, unseeing eyes staring up at the clear sky.

He'd been so fucking young. Twenty-three, just a newbie filling in spaces in shifts, cooking or riding along at the different fire stations, about to find his place. All it had taken was one lapse in judgement, one call he shouldn't have had to make.

Of course Jace was dreaming about it now. The memorial

for Hans was two days ago—the day before the divorce judgement. As a fire chief, and the acting supervisor, he'd had to attend and keep it together all day long.

He'd had to shake the hands of Hans's family members and thank them for his sacrifice, for his bravery and humor and hard work.

The whole time, Jace had hated every inch of himself.

If it weren't for him, Hans might be alive. Maybe under Chief McGregor or Chief Jackson, Hans might be alive. The better chiefs he knew in other districts, or had followed after, could have handled it.

The investigation wasn't yet complete, but Hans's death was a weight for him alone to bear. Even if the investigation found him not at fault, it was a weight he'd never be able to escape. No amount of fact-finding could change it.

Jace lay awake for a long time. The dawn was peeking through the cracks in his blinds before his eyes finally drifted shut.

"Hey, Chief."

The casual way his men still greeted him made Jace smile. Liam was one of his favorites—not that he had favorites.

Then, his heart hurt.

Hans had greeted him that way—with the same implicit trust in Jace to keep him safe. And he'd failed.

It was hard to overstate how much it affected him. Every day, he thought about it. Every hour. Not every minute, at least. He was finding some kind of weird balance among the ruins of his life. Weeks later, he was anxious and depressed, sure, but not a slow motion train wreck.

"What can I do for you?" Jace added.

"Uh, I have... some news, actually." Liam sounded proud. Had he missed some round of promotions? Christ, what *had* he missed in these weeks? Too much, no doubt.

"Shoot."

"Dylan and I are engaged."

It took a second to sink in through Jace's hazy thinking. Since his shift schedule had lapsed, he'd been under that constant fog, with no pressures to keep him to his orderly schedule. Getting up at a certain time, cooking breakfast, going for a walk—everything had to fit around his unpredictable sleep.

But the sharp, piercing joy that made his lips curl up instinctively made that haze glow in his chest, at least, for a few moments. His first thought was always, *I remember when Mike and I...* But he stopped that in its tracks.

"Oh! Wow. Congratulations! When?"

All the words he was supposed to say; at least with this long off the job, he hadn't lost his composure. None of them let slip the rest of the feelings sizzling at a low roar in his chest.

Happiness was there, yes, but also... jealousy. Yeah, that was the word.

Not that he wanted a guy quite like Dylan—the sweet, pretty boy who had utterly captivated Liam and turned him into the awkward high school class jock whenever he was around.

Not Liam himself, one of his best guys, roguish but loyal, a quick wit, and endlessly patient.

Not Chris, finally settled and seriously dating since that time at the hospital, only a month ago now. Chris was the prankster, too often let his mouth run, but at his heart he was every bit as loyal as Liam. The pair were brothers in spirit, not just on the job.

Not Ash, the soulful, sweet man Chris had saved off the

job, after an abrupt meeting with the sidewalk from his hotel window. He was a good match for Chris, with retorts he always seemed to tuck under his tongue for fear of reprisal from others, but perfectly willing to dish them out at Chris when needed.

No, his guys were perfect for each other. He was truly happy for them all. It wasn't jealousy *of* them, but of... himself? Of what he could have had?

Of what Jace *had* had, if Mike hadn't been so fucking stubborn...

Liam was talking fast, explaining how he'd taken Dylan out for a cliffside pony ride and picnic at sunset and popped the question then.

Despite the bittersweet envy welling up in his chest, Jace couldn't help but be happy for them.

"That sounds perfect for him," Jace interrupted at last, laughing quietly. "I'm really glad for you."

Jace had pushed them together, completely by accident. He'd seen those signs—the reckless hookups, the resistance to talk about them, the strange way his face shut down when the guys talked about sex sometimes... He'd almost threatened Liam into therapy.

And then something had changed. Jace still didn't know exactly *what* had changed Liam, or when, but he'd been changing slowly into a better version of himself. Especially once he'd met Dylan.

*Now I need someone to push me at someone who's actually good for me.*

"So, um, that brings me to my question! Sorry. I just talked your ear off," Liam laughed, sounding sheepish.

Jace grinned. "Oh, it's getting lonely without you guys to shout orders at."

"Quiet without you, too."

It was only a second of silence between them on the phone line, but Jace appreciated what it meant.

"So, would you help at our wedding?"

Jace hadn't expected to be a groomsman, or usher, or whatever he wanted him to do, ever again. Not that he was much older than Liam and Dylan, but...

Their friends were all partnered and figuring out how to deal with him and Mike as single guys who were courteous toward each other in court, but didn't want to see each other ever again.

Hell, he had nothing else to do until the committee's investigation was concluded.

"Yeah. I'd love to. But, uh, why not Chris? And Ash?"

"That's it, Chief. They will be helping, but..." Liam dropped his voice.

Jace could picture the way he sneakily looked around. His sheer projection often broadcasted his voice around the firehouse, even if his pitch was low. Goofball.

"But?" he prompted.

"Rumor has it... *unsubstantiated* rumor, which you didn't hear from me... that it might be a double wedding. At very short notice."

"A double..." It took Jace a second to grasp the meaning. "Oh. Oh! But they aren't even...?"

"Yet. Chris knows when he wants to—uh, allegedly has a plan."

"So Ash is the one out of the loop?"

"And Dylan. Can't risk him getting giggly and spilling the beans." Liam chuckled. "So, we need a best man."

Jace smiled softly. It made him happy to see how deeply the four had connected. Not only did they clearly love their boyfriends—fiancés in certain cases now—but they had made friends with each other, too. Dylan and Ash were now about as good friends as Liam and Chris always had been.

"So you guys need help from other people to pull it off."

"Exactly."

Jace whistled through his front teeth, but already, the prospect had him intrigued.

Maybe this could be the touch of order in his life he needed to get it all back on track.

"I'd love to. Thank you for asking me."

Liam let out a breath of relief. "Thanks, Chief. We're going to rope one of Ash's friends into being the other best man. That way, Ash and Dylan won't have a clue until the last minute. So, here's the plan."

"So much for top-secret," Jace teased.

Liam laughed. "Yeah, yeah. So, Ash is doing this hang-gliding thing, right?"

Jace searched his brain for a memory of this. Something came up, some excited puppy love rambling from Chris. He couldn't remember now. "His what?"

"Charity hang-gliding for a male suicide charity. Once he's healed."

"His leg?" In his suicide attempt, Ash had broken his leg pretty badly. He used a cane now. Honestly, Jace hadn't even known it was possible to hang-glide if you couldn't run and jump off a cliff or something.

"That's it. The date's the sixteenth of December. So, Chris is going to propose, then ask if he wants to get married, like, right away. *If* Ash is on board with the idea... which I don't see why he wouldn't be..."

"Breathe," Jace laughed. Liam was caught up in the idea now. He could see the two guys now, heads together at the coffee table in the station, scribbling plans and high-fiving.

"Right. He'll pop the question then."

"When's the wedding?"

"Uh. The twenty-first."

Some mental math meant...

"Not even a week after the proposal." Jace hummed, then nodded. "Ash will love it."

"Yes! Exactly."

It would send Jace screaming for the hills if someone suggested a week-long engagement to him, but Ash already acted like he was married to Chris. It sounded like Ash didn't have any family to invite, so if he wanted to elope... it was all up to him.

Jace recognized the bond Chris and Ash had, just like Dylan and Liam's. Every time they looked at each other, the two of them shared so much. They all *knew* already. They just had to admit it to themselves and each other. Liam and Dylan just had, at last.

Another painful twinge ripped through Jace's chest.

"I know it's around Christmas, so if you're busy with family stuff—" Liam hastily started.

*Oh, God, yes. I can get away from that!* If he hadn't been sold, he was now.

"No, I'm not. That's... Sure. I'd love that." Jace didn't know how to begin to explain the situation, the whole mess of divorcee Christmas, without bringing down the mood, so he didn't. "Thanks for thinking of me."

"Thank you!" Liam exclaimed. "Can we meet up in person, then? Go over the details? Introduce you to the other best man?"

Jace needed something to keep his mind off the waves of nervous, twitchy energy that had kept him in the house for too long. Helping make these guys' day perfect? Right up his alley.

"Set the time and place. I'll be there."

4

CHARLIE

These days, Charles spent most of his Sunday afternoons having coffee with someone. Usually, he and Ash talked over a cup of coffee, and more recently, Dylan had started coming along.

Instead of his usual two companions, though, it was their boyfriends. He'd only met Liam and Chris a couple times before, so he was nervous enough that he showed up on time—early, even.

Charles couldn't believe they'd asked him to be a best man, of all people. Of course, when he heard the reasoning, he'd instantly agreed. Nobody could pass up the chance to organize this kind of a surprise for Ash.

They'd just come off shift. Even he could see the slight tiredness in the way the firefighters carried themselves as they came into the coffee shop, looking around.

"Over here," he flagged them down with a napkin.

There was a third man with them, too.

*Who on earth is he?*

Oh, God. This wasn't the other best man, was he? Because Charles had no idea why, but the sight of him *rankled*.

Even the way the man sat as he slid in across the booth made Charles suppress a shudder. All controlled, coiled muscle and heat. The second the other man sat down, he straightened out the napkin in front of him.

On the other hand... Charles hadn't had a guy to toy with in a while. Sometimes a good old-fashioned flirt could come from the most annoying kind of guy, the one who rubbed you wrong.

And Charles wasn't in a position to be picky.

"This is Fire Chief Jace Williams," Chris was saying, and fuck, Charles hadn't the slightest idea if he'd been saying something else before. A fire chief? Yes, please. That probably meant muscles and a take-charge attitude.

He made direct eye contact with those gorgeous, light blue eyes. It took a moment to notice the crinkled frown on the other man's face as he nodded slightly.

What did he see? An average guy with surfer hair, sprawled out enough to take up one side of the booth almost entirely, tearing his napkin to shreds? And scattering the pieces across the table like an art display? Charles ripped up the last few pieces and dusted his hands off.

"And this is Charles Bryan, Ash's good friend. And, soon, his hang-gliding instructor," Chris finished.

Jace's brows rose. "Ah. Hello." He reached across the table to shake hands.

Charlie pushed the shredded napkin to the side before he took the handshake so his sleeve didn't scatter them everywhere, at least. "Hey."

That crackle between them was *not* his imagination. And not static electricity, with the humidity like it was today. Oh, no.

Jace was desperately trying not to make a comment about the napkin. He could tell already.

At least there were a couple mutual friends to defuse the moment.

"And we don't want to dump you guys here and run, but we have to talk suits with this guy we know for just, like, twenty minutes. We'll be back ASAP," Liam chimed in.

Jace's murmur was quiet. "Oh, God."

At the same moment, Charles thought, *They better not be trying to pair us off.*

Charlie caught the frown of annoyance on the chief's face, though, and suddenly his thoughts on the matter changed. *Although cracking this guy's composure would be fun. Like a nut.*

It was the thrill of the chase. That was all.

"No problem," Jace said lightly to them and raised a hand as the other two sprinted out of the coffee shop.

They both watched them jog down the sidewalk, and at the same moment, turned to face each other again.

"...So." It was Jace who spoke first, his hands folded neatly on the table. "I'll just order something. Do you..." He eyed the napkin Charlie had just shredded, to his annoyance. "Do you, uh, need anything else? Another napkin?"

Charlie glanced down at his half-full coffee mug. "Nope. Thanks." He didn't want to owe coffee to a guy he was almost certain was going to merely tolerate him and vice versa. Or even a napkin.

When the chief returned, he looked a little more relaxed as he slid into the booth again, tightly gripping his mug. "So, how long have you been hang-gliding?"

"As opening lines go, unique for you but not for me," Charlie teased. "Seven years."

Jace snorted with amusement. "Well, they didn't leave us

much to work with. If I didn't know better..." He eyed Charlie, then shook his head as he looked down. "But, no."

"Ouch." Charlie didn't even have to feign the sting.

Chief Williams looked up seconds later, his hands outspread in a quick apology. "What? No. I mean, you're not ugly."

Maybe he didn't know how to flirt. One of those tightly wound-up guys. Yeah, Charlie could handle that. He opted for the teasing route. "You're doing better and better."

"Don't fish for compliments," Jace told him, a glint in his eye now. He was playing along. "That's not attractive."

"But where would I be without my ego?" Charlie clicked his tongue. "Not running the best-ranked gliding school in the city."

Jace looked impressed, but then he lifted his eyebrow. "What kind of flight? With other people or alone?"

"Tandem's mostly for beginners, but I teach it. I go solo."

"I've been single for a while, too," Jace said and smirked, lifting a brow as he sipped his coffee.

*Hey.* Charlie glared. He was perfectly used to people assuming he was some broke surfer loser funding an extended young adulthood here on the beach. "I'll have you know I bring all the boys to my launch pad. Usually not at once."

"Mmm. Is a fear of heights a deal-breaker for you, then?" Jace grinned. "A lot of people are afraid of them, aren't they?"

"Nah. I don't care, as long as I get to ride whenever I want." *No, stop flirting. Fuck.* "Why? Did you want to fly sometime?" Charlie raised his brow.

"I think I'll leave it to the experts," Jace said, raising his cup in a slight ironic toast and sipping.

Maybe it wasn't chemistry between them, it was... barely-veiled cattiness. Was Jace the judgemental, slut-shaming type?

For his part, Jace was seeing right through to what would annoy him and happily pressing those buttons.

It flustered Charles. He couldn't remember if anyone had gotten to him like this before. He wrapped his hands tightly around his mug to calm himself again.

"So, how's fire around here?" Charlie asked, hoping to turn the heat back on him for a moment.

Jace paused, coolly evaluating him. For what, Charlie wasn't sure. Then, he nodded. "Quiet for me. I've been on leave for a while."

"Oh." Charlie couldn't really make fun of that. He winced. "Sorry?"

"Don't be," Jace said, but there was tightly-controlled emotion there. Everything with him felt tightly-controlled, really. It made Charlie itch just talking to him. God help whoever he wound up dating. "Just an admin leave. Standard procedure after incidents."

"Ahh." Charlie remembered Ash saying something about a memorial, and... wait, this guy was a chief? He'd been involved? Shit, had he gotten some guy killed? He remembered Ash talking about a memorial not long ago, too. Very recently.

Jace was watching him closely, but no reactions showed themselves. Charlie couldn't tell if he'd been broadcasting his thoughts on his face like usual. He tried not to recoil.

"Right," Charlie added to make it clear he wasn't gonna say anything about that. "More time for you to... do other things?"

"I don't have a lot of hobbies." Jace didn't sound apologetic or giggly like some guys would when they said that. He was honest, then, and blunt with what he did say, even if it wasn't much. Strong and silent? Charlie's type.

"Oh. Maybe you'd have more boys in *your* yard if you did," Charlie smirked.

"I'm off the market for a few months."

*He's not married, is he?* Charlie had seen it all—guys who played the women they were with by going out of town for work, juggling partners carefully. That could explain his weird reticence. "That's... very specific."

"It is." Jace's tone made it clear he wasn't going to talk about that.

Well, damn. This conversation was hard.

Charles wasn't going to push against a brick wall, even if the terrible part of him that knew he shouldn't be turned on by guys who weren't *right* for him was... really fucking turned on.

Not just physically. Emotional walls were even more tempting for him to crack. And then there was the worry... if he didn't do *something* to make it clear that there were no bonds available, would one form? It made him itch to think about.

Whenever Jace shifted, the light showed the muscles under his thin t-shirt, and he *was* a brick wall. Charles wanted to picture himself being shoved up against a wall by this hunk, but it was hard to imagine it vividly when he couldn't picture Jace's self-control breaking. Yet.

God, this was the last thing he needed. *Don't start fucking guys you don't like just to keep them from crushing on you. Also, don't fuck your friends' friends.*

"So, the wedding date. We gotta start working backward from there," Charlie said abruptly, pulling his phone out to take notes on what Jace knew—which wasn't much more than him. They only knew they had to plan the bachelor party ASAP.

True to their word, and thank *God* for the break in the tension, Chris and Liam came back just then, so they got the answers they were looking for.

Most of them, anyway.

Jace maintained that same careful, cool tone the whole time, even after Chris and Liam came back. There was no hint as to *why* Jace was off the market, or what they'd been thinking leaving the two of them alone.

After they wound up their meeting and Charlie walked toward his car, his chest was tight. It was hard seeing Chris and Liam be so damn happy about their wedding. He was happy for them, sure, but... he sort of resented it, too.

Which was stupid. Just because *he* didn't want strings, he had no right to be jealous of those who did and were happy with them. This was his chance to be a bigger man and put up with a little romance, for once.

"Put up or shut up," he mumbled to himself as he shielded his eyes from the sun and trotted across the street to his car. *Or put my legs up. Choose one.*

And he sure as hell didn't know anyone he wanted to put up for in either way.

5

---

JACE

"Jace Williams?"

He knew that voice.

Still, Jace kept his shoulders down and expression calm when speaking into the phone. Body language carried to the voice over a radio channel or phone line.

"That's me. How can I help?"

"It's Roger Dunworth here." Just as he'd thought, the leader of the inquiry into Hans's death. Jace's heart was already hammering, even though he knew Roger wasn't going to give him anything over the phone. "Are you free for a meeting? I don't want to worry you, but understandably, your boss wants to go over the results of the inquiry internally before we announce anything to the public."

This sounded like bad news, however he tried to pitch it. Jace could feel his blood pressure spiking already as he glanced around for the DVD player clock, then remembered Mike had taken it. He rolled his eyes and looked at the living room wall clock instead.

It was early enough that maybe he'd just got to work—five

past eight. Jace furrowed his brows. "I'm free this morning. I have a quick thing with a friend in the early afternoon, but I can reschedule it if need be—"

"No, no. Morning would be better," Roger told him. "I should have time in advance to take care of things."

Things like meeting up with his boss to brief him ahead of time? Still, he was going to face the music no matter what.

He might be a wreck afterward, but he shouldn't blow off Charlie today when they were about to plan the bachelor party. That was only next weekend.

Liam's, of course, since Chris and Ash weren't yet engaged. If they even had a bachelor party, it would be a lot smaller. Chris said he was fine with that, and Ash wasn't big on partying these days, anyway.

"Right, of course. What time?" He couldn't feel his hands. He gripped the phone so hard he heard it squeak against the edge of his case.

"Is ten fine?"

"Ten works. Thanks for letting me know..." Jace trailed off.

There was no hint of an answer to his unspoken question in Roger's voice. "I'll see you then."

Jace swallowed everything he wanted to ask. He wasn't going to lose his dignity and beg for answers now. He just bade Roger goodbye for now, struggling to get the full breath out, then hung up.

Finally, he let himself double over to catch his breath. The blood rushed to his head, and sparks crackled at the edges of his vision.

It was a process he was familiar with now. He dropped onto the floor, before it could get worse.

*I'm going to be let go. My name will be everywhere. Everyone will know it was me who let him down.*

*Worst of all: it was me who caused this.*

*It's my fault he's dead. Or I could have done more. Something. Anything.*

"Shut up," Jace breathed out at his thoughts.

The mandated post-incident therapy sessions had lasted about a month. Not terribly helpful. Mostly, they'd gone over the process of integrating trauma into his consciousness, or whatever.

Well, he didn't need help with that. He knew it had happened. Logically, he knew it wasn't his fault. He didn't have any abnormal symptoms—trauma symptoms would have to persist for a few more months before it qualified as PTSD, anyway.

But it didn't stop this irrational, animal instinct from grabbing him by the throat at seemingly random moments.

He'd Googled it. It wasn't a flashback—he didn't find himself reliving the moments of the fire any more than he did consciously. Reenacting everything that had happened was normal.

It wasn't a phobia, nothing specific brought it on.

He...

Just. Couldn't. Breathe.

He was on his side on the floor, his nails biting into his palms, phone forgotten. He wanted to find something to hide under, or behind, like a little kid.

Jace focused on his breathing, the blood rushing through his body, tensing all his muscles. He was shaking, too—it took him until now to notice. Had he been shaking the whole time, or only now?

He crunched his eyes closed as the tide washed him away. He was struggling in the surf against the immenseness of... his own brain. Physically, he could feel his body on the floor, but mentally, he was gone.

This was a bad one. Logically, he knew it. There were small

ones, where he breathed fast for a while and felt jittery, and there were big ones. Thankfully, they all eventually ended.

It didn't feel like this one did, though. It felt like this one was *the last one* he would ever experience, because it might just kill him. Somehow, he was never going to be free of it.

No, that was untrue. He always was. The therapist had talked over it with him. He was supposed to challenge thoughts of doom and gloom, so that was exactly what he did.

*I don't know who's at fault. I'm going to make it through, somehow, even if I am. I can make an example of this, at least, and help keep others safe. I'll find a way to do it.*

And he focused on his breathing.

Breathing and thinking—that was all he could manage. He couldn't tell how long it took.

When his eyes drifted open and he found himself staring at the TV on one side, the couch on the other, he realized where he was.

Home. The living room floor. Lying there, staring at the ceiling, his chest finally loosening.

And he was throbbing in his jeans, achingly hard.

Fuck. Not again.

It had happened a couple times—only during the worst attacks. Unconscious response to the tension clamping every muscle, the blood pumping hard through his body.

Jace *could* think of a quick way to relax, though. He unzipped his jeans and slid his hand inside, palming his shaft.

Fucking hell, he was just about on the edge. How long had he been like this, achingly desperate and tense without even the self-consciousness to know it?

His heart sank like a stone. He'd gone through this before. Something like it, anyway. Before Mike, he'd tried to fuck away his problems, and no amount of sex had cut through the fear and anxiety that controlled him.

Only facing his own demons had stopped it. It was why he'd known Liam needed help.

But here he was, again, desperately filling the cracks in the walls between him and *that*, fending it off at every turn.

"Fuck it."

Jace pushed down his jeans, gripping his shaft and stroking hard. He was damp, precum already leaking down his cock. "Yes... *Yes*," he grunted, his head rolling back against the floor.

Finally, something he could enjoy, just for himself. Something to take his mind off everything he was drowning in.

His fist tight, teeth gritted, Jace could nearly imagine a gorgeous guy riding him, knees to the carpet, bouncing up and down...

*This* was the kind of tension his body liked. The kind with a promise of orgasm at the end, and the visuals of a pretty guy.

Jace hadn't hooked up in so long, he barely knew how to picture some random hookup, and his brain helpfully supplied someone he knew instead. The least weird... or most, depending on his perspective... Charles?

They didn't get along. That much was obvious. But he *was* gorgeous. Longer hair, just long enough to get into his eyes, but not a guy trying to look twenty. A certain confidence about him —the knowledge and self-possession to know who he was and where he was going.

An attitude, too. He'd sniped back just as much as Jace had. Oh, he knew his mind, all right. Infuriatingly so, perhaps. He'd deliberately fidgeted with everything on the table after noticing Jace straightening it out.

And he'd hit on him so hard Jace's head had nearly spun. He'd forgotten what it was like to be pursued like that. Charles had let it go when Jace had hinted he wasn't interested, but that hadn't stopped them eye-fucking for the rest of the coffee date.

Charles also had a *great* ass. Jace had noticed him walking out to his car, all right. He wouldn't mind getting a handful of that, grabbing him, pushing him up against the wall. Punishing him for taunting him.

Grabbing Charles's wrists while his muscled body rose and fell above him and rode him hard. Making Charles beg to touch his own aching, swollen dick as it bounced above his stomach. Pushing his hips up to grind against the sweet spot inside until Charles howled with need and pleasure.

Drinking in every expression of Charles's ecstasy as he threw his head back, and—

"*Yes!*" Jace grunted hard, slamming his hips up into his fist as he came. "Fuck... fuck! Fuck, Charles, yes..."

Now his shirt was sticky, but he was boneless, the tension draining as his heart rate slowed to normal, or even slower. He could almost sleep on the floor.

*Oh, boy.* He didn't usually go for names. Christ. When was the last time he'd *used* someone's name, other than Mike's? He drew a blank.

Maybe there was a spark of chemistry every time they touched, a sizzle of attraction between them, but he didn't have to acknowledge it.

Besides, he had bigger things on his mind.

Like going to see him.

"Of course I would," Jace muttered. He had to look Charles in the eye without flinching, or Charles would know he was getting to him—one way or another.

And if it was sexual... Jace wasn't sure he was strong enough to say no. Even if, from this limited first impression, he was convinced they *were* totally wrong for each other.

*Opposites attract.*

## 6

## CHARLIE

Charles didn't even *like* the guy, let alone plan to have him over long enough to cook for him. Why the fuck was he cleaning his kitchen cupboards?

He blew out an exhausted sigh and slammed the last cupboard shut. The damn kitchen smelled like lemon now. It was all Jace's damn fault. Not that Jace knew it yet.

He was supposed to be here any minute to talk bachelor parties, and knowing him, even from having met him once, Charles had the feeling he'd show up five minutes early.

Which meant he had to be ready even earlier, and... he still smelled like cleaner.

"Shit."

Charles unlocked the front door, then pulled back the curtain to check. No cars, no ridiculously attractive fussy men striding up the sidewalk. He might have time.

He made a beeline for the shower, stripping his clothes as he went and bundling them under his arm. He nearly crashed through the bathroom door when he got his jeans around his knees, but managed to hip-check it open and step out of his pants.

"That'll bruise," he muttered, peeling them off his feet and tossing the whole bundle in the laundry basket.

The first blast of hot water across his skin was a welcome relief. Cleaning was such a damn pain. He wasn't a slob, but he also didn't dust his cabinets as often as Martha Stewart would.

He tried not to waste time, but holy fuck, the flight yesterday had been a bad one. He'd been battling buffeting, uneven winds with a newbie, trying to keep it level and smooth for her. And then they'd landed pretty rough. The water beating into his sore shoulders was divine.

Charles rubbed his soap bar across his palms, then wiped his face and neck clean, his eyes sliding shut. There was nothing like a good shower and some alone time to get his mind focused again before Jace came over.

Oh, Jace. Charles didn't even know why the man got to him so much, except for having such an opposite personality.

Well, no, that wasn't true. It reminded him of every fussy teacher, of his grandparents, of everyone who'd grated his nerves throughout his life and told him to get a real office job. To Jace's credit, he hadn't asked *that* of him yet, but Charles felt like it was only a matter of time.

Maybe it was the man's penchant for details—he'd interrupted Charles at least three times the last and only time they'd met, at the coffee shop, to take notes. He needed everything in order and written down and neatly stored away. That stifled Charles's creativity. He'd forgotten a damn good reception party idea because of him.

Sure, he couldn't remember now what the idea had been, but he was sure it was a good one.

He grumbled under his breath, trying not to let his mind

wander to the man's perfect pink lips and closed-off eyes. How fucking fun would it be to make him lose control? To crash on the bed, legs spread, and give him the come-hither look until he moaned with desire?

Charles's shaft was hard already, hot water dripping from the tip as he half-idly fondled it, almost without thinking. It was such a natural gesture, especially living alone as he did. He preferred someone else's hand on it, but it would do.

*Uh oh. Better do it or kill it.*

Charles hadn't had time for much *else* that day, between tidying his place and getting groceries. And he was going to pay for it, if Jace hung around being an attractive nuisance and making him want to smash him up against a wall and undo his inhibitions, along with...

No, he *really* didn't have time. Jace was going to be there literally any minute.

Charles groaned, his body already tensing in anticipation as he turned his hips away from the stream of water, trying to ease out of it as much as possible, and turned the tap to cold.

The yelp he let out was fucking undignified, but he had every right.

*That* worked, if nothing else, to draw his attention back to the very pressing problem of getting out, dried off, and dressed again before Jace showed up on his doorstep wondering where he was.

"Sorry, buddy," he muttered under his breath. "We'll have time for that later."

He turned the tap handle back to lukewarm, but he was still shivering as he poured shampoo in his palm, rubbed it through his hair, and rinsed the soap from the rest of his body with his other hand.

It was, of fucking *course*, exactly then that Jace rang the doorbell. Or someone, but he could only assume he knew who it was.

"Come in!" he yelled, blinking and praying he wasn't about to get two eyes full of shampoo.

Charles heard a voice from the other side of the door. It was indistinct but enough to make out the tone. It had to be Jace.

Good thing he *hadn't* just gone to town on himself.

"Come in," he repeated, a little louder.

Another voice, but still from outside, and no sound of the front door opening.

"Oh, Jesus fuck," he groaned. There was no way this wasn't gonna be awkward. And Jace probably wouldn't let him live it down. He brushed his hand back through his forehead and hair to make sure he wasn't about to blind himself, then shut off the water.

It took just a second to wrap the towel around his waist. Charles tucked it in extra-carefully, then had a quick glance down just to make sure everything was in order.

It was definitely Jace, judging by the size and shape of the man on the other side of the glass window in the door. Still grumbling under his breath, Charles yanked on the doorknob, already starting to say, "I *said*—"

Something in his shoulder wrenched.

"Oh, *fuck*."

He almost doubled over, catching his breath as the shooting pain ran from his neck down his shoulder.

He'd forgotten the second lock on the door when he unlocked it. That explained why Jace hadn't let himself in.

When he clicked it open, Jace shouldered his way in. "Fuck. I saw that. Are you okay? Jesus, be careful!"

Charles grunted his annoyance and stood back for Jace to pass. "I don't need a lecture on being careful in my own damn home." He was still leaning on the edge of the door, though, processing the ache and cataloging it.

Just a pull the wrong way. By far not the worst he'd had. Good. He shouldn't have to cancel any appointments. It'd get better in a day or two.

Warm, broad hands were on Charles's shoulder, pulling him away from the door and closing it. Without thinking twice, he leaned into the hold as the sharp starbursts of pain scraped his nerves.

Jace smelled good. Clean, solid. A touch of... spice? Cinnamon? Not cigars, but maybe tobacco? He was wearing something that was probably meant for a nightclub, but Charles didn't have it in him to form a snarky comment.

Also, he was half-naked, still wet, leaning into Jace like he was coming on to him, and... shit! Shampoo was running into his eyes. And... his towel was slipping.

"Son of a *bitch*." Charles yelped and swiped at his eyes, pushing away from Jace and stumbling for the bathroom while he grabbed for his towel with the other hand.

"Watch—there's a wall—" Jace started.

Charles ignored him. "Fucking cocknugget, you Paul Mitchell fucker, and your fucking awapuhi torture fuckery." Tears streamed down his face as he bounced off the door frame, then stumbled through on his way to the shower. "And fuck these tiny fucking IKEA towels."

Jace's laugh was rich. It seemed to fill every nook and cranny as it came rolling through the front hall after him. Charles couldn't even see where Jace was going, but he trusted he'd make himself at home.

But Jace was leaning on the other side of the door after he closed it, judging by how clear his voice was. "If that was you trying to come on to me, I think you're supposed to rinse out the shampoo before you answer the door. The half-naked, wet look suits you, though."

Charles flipped off the door as his towel dropped to the floor, trying to ignore how damn *hot* the prospect of Jace just shouldering his way through *this* door made him.

His cock was not supposed to spring into action when his eyeballs were about to burn out of his fucking skull.

*Thanks again, Paul Mitchell. I'm blaming that on you, too.*

"I wasn't coming on to you," Charles retorted, turning on the bath faucet and dropping to his knees for a quick blast of water.

"I'll write it off as a mismatch in, er... timeliness," Jace teased.

Charles's shoulder still ached from the yank he'd given it, but it was the last thing on his dick's mind. "Fuck off. I was cleaning." God, his nerves were already prickling, and he *wished* his cock weren't, too.

He dunked his head under the hot running water, so he didn't hear Jace's response.

A few rinses later, gasping, Charles emerged from the water, shut off the handle, and grabbed for his towel to dab his hair dry. Of course he didn't have his change of clothes in here, so he'd have to wrap the towel around his waist again to head through to his bedroom.

Charles expected some smart-ass comment from Jace, but heard nothing. He had to stop for a moment and look at himself in the steamy bathroom mirror before he made the run. He adjusted the knot in his towel, pushed his hair back just so, and rubbed his cheeks. No time to shave now.

But that didn't matter. Not like he was trying to impress Jace, of all people. He just wanted to get through today without killing him.

He strode quickly through the hall to his bedroom, grateful that he heard a rattling sound from the kitchen.

"Good thing I *did* clean," he called as he pushed his bedroom door open. "If you're looking for soda, it's in the fridge."

"Thanks." Jace stuck his head around the doorway, and then his eyes slid slowly up and down Charles's body. He didn't make a secret about it, but he wasn't completely serious, either. His smirk was teasing.

Charles tried not to heat up with pleasure at the once-over. Fucking hell, he needed to get laid, even if he had to put up with some clingy weirdo for it. Now he was getting all horny just because some hot, muscled hunk with a smarmy attitude was in his living room.

The reasonable part of his brain pointed out that it wasn't just Jace being smarmy. Charles didn't know who had really started it. They both rubbed each other up exactly the wrong way, seemingly as naturally as breathing.

Jace lowered his voice to a sultry purr, his grin wicked. "Not coming on to me, huh?"

The spell was broken. Charles flipped him off and shoved his way into his bedroom, kicking the door shut behind him as Jace's laughter echoed.

---

"So, how's your day been?"

It was only supposed to be a casual question as they looked through Google Maps on their phones, both fully-dressed now and sitting opposite one another on the armchair and the sofa.

But Jace's flinch, as much as he tried to hide it, was obvious.

Charles's stare was drawn from his screen back to the other man, who filled up so much space with his very presence, let alone his physical frame. Had to be six-something, pure muscle and energy and quiet, steely focus.

Contrast to Charles's own body—lithe, thin, muscled where it counted but otherwise efficient for flight.

Jace could wrap him up from behind and blanket him perfectly.

*Whoa.* That *train of thought can fuck off.*

"Had better," Jace said simply, in a tone of voice that suggested he didn't feel like saying more. He was giving Charles an assessing look, like he wasn't sure if he was safe talking to him about it. He quickly looked back at his phone.

Charles's heart sank. It was a lot less fun needling him now that he knew he was genuinely upset, unless it would help him get his mind off it. It was hard to know how to respond without knowing what was going on, but he gave the guy a sympathetic look. "Yeah? Shitty. Sorry."

Jace seemed surprised for a moment, his gaze flickering up to meet Charles's. Then he winked. "Don't be too nice. I might like you, if you aren't careful."

The flirtation made Charles's heart rate rise. Nothing serious, just playing around. *This* was what he didn't mind. He felt his cheeks heat up as he grinned back. "Can't risk that. I won't make a habit of it."

"Good." Jace swigged his Coke and waved his phone at him. "I think this place will work. I've been there a couple times."

The lounge he'd chosen seemed like Liam's kind of place, and a good spot for a small party. "Yeah. Yeah, that's good." Charles set his soda aside and leaned over the coffee table, reaching through the space between them to take his phone and look at the photos.

Their hands brushed, and Charles stifled his quick gasp. Jace was still on the other side of the coffee table, but the brush of the sides of his fingers against Charles's hand had made him feel a lot closer.

Now, that was fucking *weird*.

He focused hard on the space: nice lighting, table reservations for small groups like theirs, and good Yelp scores. "We should check it out tonight," Charles suggested. He'd been there before—what gay bar in the area hadn't he been to?—but it had been a while.

"Yeah." Jace took back his phone, then glanced at it. "I have a shortlist of five bars selected, but this one should meet all our criteria. We'll start there."

Charles almost rolled his eyes but barely managed not to. "One should be enough, if it's the right one." It seemed like a waste of time and energy to look up more.

"I have a meeting this afternoon, but I'm free in the evening."

"Tonight works for me. I'll text you a time," Charles told him.

"Give me more than three seconds of notice." Jace smirked. "I've heard of your habits."

Charles groaned. "That was only once. Or twice. A few times..." he trailed off.

Well, honestly, most times he met Ash, he ran either early or late. If he came too early, he'd wander off to check out shops, get distracted, and sprint back to the cafe a little late. He was damned either way. It was hard for him to estimate how much time he needed to get to places.

"I rest my case," Jace winked, then rose to his feet. "Okay, man. See you tonight."

The clap on his shoulder and momentary strong grip was an unexpected pleasure. Despite their needling words, Jace did actually seem to be taking a shine to him, and Charles had to admit Jace was growing on him.

He still didn't *know* the guy, but maybe side-by-side at that flashy place with Jace, the fire chief would unwind a little.

If, while showing Jace out of his apartment, Charles was imagining making Jace unwind against his mouth... well, that was between him, his dick, and his half-finished shower.

## 7

## JACE

"What do you think of the music here?"

Just like he did with everything, Charles raised a shoulder in a casual half-shrug and offered a bright smile. "I'm easy."

Jace side-eyed him as he tipped his head back to down another shot. He slid the glass across the counter and made eye contact with the bartender to get another. "I think we established that earlier today."

He had no idea what it was about Charles that brought out his catty side. He was normally so cool-headed, even under tremendous pressure. Hell, he'd barely raised his voice when he kicked Mike out.

"Oof!" Charles laughed, running his thumb along the rim of his salted glass and licking it. "Reowr."

Wait. Had he actually offended him? Jace raised his hands in apology, but Charles snorted with laughter and waved it off.

Maybe it was the stress making it hard to judge what was Charles joking back with him and what wasn't. That fucking meeting.

But he was ready to put the meeting out of mind. He still

had a job, and he wasn't in trouble. Whether or not he agreed with their conclusions, Jace had already decided not to think about it until tomorrow. He was out to have fun tonight.

Charles's easygoing approach was exactly wrong for planning this kind of event—a wedding, probably double wedding—but there was something charming about him. Something that made it possible for him to have fun throwing barbs back and forth with him.

They clearly didn't *actually* hate each other. Not for something big, like a difference in their moral compasses. And it sure beat awkward silence from some nice, sweet, quiet boy. No, Charles gave as good as he got, and it was... intriguing.

That was a good word. Not overly committed, but measured. Intriguing.

He needed another shot.

"I'm sure off-the-market men like you don't mind what their sluttier friends do," Charles added in an undertone, rolling his eyes at himself in the bar mirror.

"Did you just call yourself...?" Jace hadn't expected that from Charles, for some reason.

Charles's lips tightened and he nodded slightly. So he wasn't necessarily *happy* about getting around.

There was no way to handle it without getting touchy-feely, so Jace clapped his back and signalled the bartender for two shots. "Charlie boy," he winked.

"Oh, God. I hate that nickname."

"Perfect. Charlie boy," Jace repeated, restraining his smile. "Make up your mind about what you want and go for it. Don't let my teasing get to you."

Charles looked so startled he almost fell off his stool. "What?" He recovered and laughed, elbowing Jace. "I'm fine. I know what I want. I don't care if you think I'm easy for answering the door naked. We're just fucking around, right?"

"Good," Jace nodded, squaring away that in his mind. It was easier to banter when he knew it wasn't actually bothering Charlie... Charles? No, he preferred Charlie. "Yeah. Charlie."

The bartender raised his brows, but to his credit, made no comment as he passed over their shots.

Jace slid a bill over the counter and waved away change, then leaned on the counter and inspected Charlie.

Something about him looked... vulnerable.

There was no real evidence. He had no idea what it was that made him think that. Maybe it was projection, for fuck's sake.

But the way Charles watched him... it wasn't as closed-off as it had been the first time they'd met, or even earlier that afternoon. He hesitated as he picked up his shot, then touched it to Jace's glass and downed it.

Jace drew a breath, watching the other man's Adam's apple slide up and down, then closed his eyes and threw his head back to let the burning liquid slide down his throat.

But it wasn't his turn under the spotlight.

"So, what's wrong?" Charles asked, quieter this time. "If you want to tell some random dick like me."

"Not totally random. My guys trust you," Jace said simply. And he'd trust Liam and Chris with his life again, as he had in the past.

That reminded him of—but *no*.

Plus, Dylan and Ash seemed like pretty solid judges of character, and they liked Charles, too. It was just the tardiness and spacey attitude that made Jace roll his eyes, and Mike had always been on him not to be so uptight.

*Let it go, man. Takes all types to make up the world.*

Jace drew a breath and let it out, then shrugged slightly. "Just had a meeting about work. I don't want to discuss it. And I just ended a long-term relationship a few months ago."

"Oh. Ouch." Charlie winced, gazed at Jace for a second, then punched his shoulder. "Next shot's on me. And we're dancing later."

Jace groaned. "I don't need your pity shot," he protested, but he didn't stop Charles flagging down the bartender for another.

The club music was loud, the lights bright. The thumping bass reverberated through his body, making his toes curl into the ground.

So long with Mike that he'd forgotten what the scene felt like. And it felt *good*. It felt... like he used to feel.

He used to be more carefree, before he'd been made chief. Before he had responsibilities, and Mike, and everything weighing down on his mind.

His new—friend? Frenemy?—leaned into him. "Fewer strings to a pity shot than a pity fuck," he murmured, his voice just a bare growl over the thumping dance line in Jace's ear.

And despite himself, Jace prickled with heat. Every fucking time he made those eyes at him, it stirred his nerves. He paused a second before rolling his eyes in an imitation of Charlie.

Charlie's grin of recognition and mock outrage was quick. He kicked Jace's stool, then slid his shot to him, tapped glasses, and downed his.

It occurred to Jace as he was letting the whiskey run down the back of his throat that it was easier to attribute his interest in Charles to dislike than like. Dislike was safe and fun. Like was risky and fun. He wasn't keen on risk.

The corners of Jace's eyes prickled with hot tears as he drew a quick breath, too stubborn to cough. Fuck, he couldn't breathe for a second.

"So, does your checklist say yes to this place?"

It took him a few seconds to realize what Charlie meant. The room was hot, and bodies brushed by a little too closely.

His nerves were on-edge, but not in an unpleasant way. Not like they had been for weeks now.

In a *good* way. In a way that made him feel alive, and here, and... happy for the momentary human connection.

Oh, fuck, he was a loser.

Jace nodded quickly. "For the thing? Yeah."

"You're not at all drunk," Charlie accused, winking. "Might need another few shots in you."

"Oh, shut up," Jace laughed. "I don't drink normally. Not before... work stuff happened. And then the breakup. Then it just seemed like a bad idea to start."

"Yeah, no breakup advice at the bottom of a bottle," Charlie agreed. Was that a glint of respect in his eyes? His hand was on Jace's knee now, his gaze sympathetic. "I'm sorry. Must be hard. How long was it?"

"Fuck off, Charlie," Jace rolled his eyes. He didn't need a pity shot, a pity fuck, *or* a pity grope. "I'm fine. Not long enough I miss it, or the guy it's attached to." He smirked and waited.

It took Charlie a second to realize there was innuendo. Then, he almost fell off his stool with laughter, gripping the edge of the counter.

Jace's lips quirked into a dirty smile as he shifted in time with the music on the stool. This was a good song. He didn't know it, but he wanted to move.

"Man, I thought you didn't have a normal sense of humor under there," Charlie finally managed. He eased himself to his feet and grabbed Jace's arm. "Come on. Dance. Let loose."

"Everyone tells me to do that," Jace grumbled, but it was a relief. Honestly, he'd expected Charlie would ditch him for some pretty little thing the moment they got there. He hadn't planned out what to say now. Dancing saved him from that.

"Then they're right." If he was a little unsteady on his feet,

Charlie had a tight grip on his arm, but Jace suspected Charlie was in a similar boat. They found a spot on the floor with enough elbow-room for two, and their chests almost brushed together.

Whoa. There went the idea of personal space or elbow room.

And Jace *liked* it.

Charles eyed him with a grin as they shimmied to the music, his hands raising. The elegance of his hands twisting in the air, the dirty little roll to his hips, the way his gaze was fixed on Jace's...

Oh, fuck. He was *definitely* coming on to him.

"You're a bad man, Charlie," Jace leaned in enough to inform him, which was close enough to smell the faint hint of cologne. Spice, floral, woodsy... something utterly intoxicating.

Charlie's hand slid up Jace's back, all the way to cup the back of his neck, making his skin prickle with pleasurable heat up from the base of his spine to his head. He was leaning in, too, their chests brushing and hips barely apart. "I'll let you get away with calling me that. Good thing I like you."

"*Excuse* you," Jace swatted his chest, giving him a punch-drunk grin. He wasn't going to risk becoming cozy little BFFs like Dylan and Ash had. Tonight was different. He wasn't going to ruin the balance of their tentative relationship. Though he hated the word... frenemies? Whatever it was, it was the first *fun* relationship he could ever remember.

"I mean, I hate you, you... uptight, fussy little prick," Charles quickly corrected himself, pressing his lips against Jace's neck.

Oh, fuck. It had been months since Mike—nobody else since then. Jace's hands found Charlie's shoulders. He moaned at the warmth against the sensitive flesh, then cleared his throat. "Excuse you. Not *little*."

The music vibrated through every inch of his core now, loud and unrelenting.

"Really?" Charlie whispered, his hands running slowly back down Jace's back toward his ass. Knowing exactly where they were going made it damn near impossible for Jace not to get a semi. "I'd like to find out."

"You're a terrible man."

Charlie winked, his hands lingering on Jace's ass as they shimmied and swayed together. "No wonder you hate me."

It was impossible not to picture himself hefting the lighter man into the air and just *slamming* him against the wall. Cheeky bastard. Jace's heart hammered as one of Charlie's hands slipped between them to pluck at his waistband.

Then, Charlie stole a quick grope. "Oh, *someone* likes me. Little-not-little Jace."

"Fuck you." Jace was laughing despite himself, pressing into Charlie's hand and grabbing his ass in return. If Charlie was going to fight dirty, well... two could play that game.

"Would you like to?"

Jace couldn't breathe. When he'd filed the divorce papers, or stood on the courthouse steps like a free man... he hadn't imagined himself in this kind of situation so quickly.

Or, truth be told, ever again.

But maybe he wasn't damaged goods. Not completely. Enough that he could fool Charlie for a while, apparently. He wouldn't want to stick around, and Jace didn't want him to, but...

The bed sounded like a great way to sort out their differences.

It was all he could think of: Charlie's smell, the feeling of his lips against Jace's bare skin, the hand that was slipping up under his t-shirt now, running up his chest.

Holy fuck. He didn't have a response prepared for this.

"Are you weighing the pros and cons?" Charlie smirked. "Making a list? Checking it twice?"

Jace blushed and pushed Charlie's chest, growling into his ear over the music as their bodies swayed together. Warm, solid. *Good.* "You're a little mouthy git."

"I take great pleasure in mouthing it."

"I said—"

Charlie's finger circled one of his nipples under his t-shirt.

In public! That was way further than... well, Mike would have done it, but Jace had never let him. But letting go was such sweet relief. Letting go of his expectations, of his grudges and the way he ordered his world, of... *everything.*

"Yes."

Charlie's hand found his, warm and strong, fingers lacing as Charlie pulled him free from the crowds on the dance floor, out the door to the warm summer evening.

Jace took stock of the situation. The first few drinks had worn off. He was sobering up, but his head still spun. Which meant it was Charlie himself having this effect on him, not alcohol, and... that was...

"Cab? Mine's fine."

Scary. Good thing he didn't walk away from scary. "Sure." Jace hardly wanted to break the stillness between them. The thumping music still leaking from the club's front door, the raised voices of the smokers gathered away from the entrance— it all blended and blurred into nothing of consequence.

He was a lot more interested in wrapping his arms around Charlie's shoulders as they waited for the taxi, their bodies swaying together. Charlie fit against his front, just a couple inches shorter, almost as broad in the shoulders, but with a narrower waist, a slender torso.

Just these few minutes of allowing themselves to cross those strictly-held lines kept his skin crackling with pleasant heat.

But Charlie was so much bolder than him. Charlie was pushing at his hand, sliding their laced fingers up under his shirt to make Jace feel him up.

Jace pulled his hand away and pinched his side. "In *public.*"

"Mmm. It happens," Charlie smirked, running his hand back down to Jace's, then placing it on his stomach again—on the outside of his shirt this time. "Better, oh shy one?"

Jace growled and pressed into Charlie's ass, angling his hips so Charlie could feel his cock slowly hardening again. He'd show him how *shy* he was.

But he had a feeling that was just what Charlie was going for. He pulled back, ignoring Charlie's stumble backward into him again and side-stepping him.

"Charlie. You're a sneaky little devil."

"I am," Charlie whispered. The taxi pulled up, and Jace kept his hand on the small of Charlie's back, as if afraid to break the spell between them.

Maybe they'd come to their senses and realize they didn't *belong* together.

But after Charlie leaned forward and gave his address, he reached across the middle of the backseat to take Jace's hand again, slowly stroking his palm with his fingers.

One more shudder of desire worked its way through Jace's whole body, toes to head.

*Just this once.*

In Jace's admittedly limited and outdated experience, the taxi ride tended to cool off passions. Maybe that was because he'd spent most of those rides carefully avoiding touching whoever he was following or bringing home. And then there'd been Mike, and not even him but also nobody else for so long.

But this time? Fuck, no.

If possible, by the time he was crowding up behind Charlie on his front step, tickling him to make him fumble with his keys, laughing as Charlie tried to elbow him away... he wanted him *more*.

But today was upside-down day. He wasn't going to question anything.

"You know, Jace... you're an ass, too," Charlie snorted. He almost fell inside. Jace knew the place well enough now to know where the bedroom was, so he shoved Charlie in that direction without even kicking his shoes off.

"Good thing I like that."

"Asses? Or mine?"

Jace grinned briefly, his eyes adjusting to the semidarkness in Charlie's room. "Yours tonight."

Earlier that day, Charlie stumbling into him, half-naked and wet, had sent a lot dirtier thoughts through his mind than he'd ever admit.

"How's your shoulder?" Jace added, closing the door behind them and following Charlie to the bed.

Charlie smirked. "I know what *you're* remembering. Perv." He swayed on his feet next to the bed, pulling his t-shirt off. When Jace took a closer look, those movements were deliberate. Charlie was as sober as Jace... he was just trying to tempt him.

And fuck, it worked.

"Well, when you're showing it all off..." Jace sidled up to Charlie and pressed their chests together, sliding his hands down Charlie's back to hook his thumbs into his waistband. "You weren't planning this, were you?" he teased.

"Hell, no. With *you*?" Charlie stuck out his tongue.

Jace's eyes flickered down to Charlie's lips. It was so tempting to lean in for a kiss, but the thought made his stomach tight. He hadn't kissed another man in... a long fucking time.

He pressed his lips to Charlie's neck instead, kissing down to his collarbone while Charlie's sighs of pleasure echoed in the quiet bedroom. Charlie tasted good—faintly salty, but there was a sweet tang to his skin.

Jace wasn't sure if Charlie pulled him down or he pushed Charlie. Either way, by unspoken mutual agreement, they were on the bed. He straddled the other man, raising his arms to let Charlie pull his shirt off.

Charlie's low whistle of appreciation made Jace grin. He put enough damn time in at the gym—why shouldn't he reap the rewards? "Like it?" he teased.

"All right," Charlie shrugged casually, but he took a few seconds to tear his eyes off Jace's chest and abs.

Jace smirked. "I'll show you *all right*." He flicked one of Charlie's nipples.

Charlie just about flipped him off, his body arched so hard. "*Fuck*! You fucking—"

"Whoa," Jace breathed, rubbing with the pad of a thumb to soothe the skin. "Someone's sensitive."

"I'll show *you* sensitive," Charlie breathed out hoarsely, and fuck, that voice was sexy. Charlie's nails dug into his shoulders, hauling him down until their bodies crashed together. Teeth were on his neck, and Charlie sucked hard on the sensitive spots he found there.

Jace couldn't help showing him where they were, too. He was hard, throbbing in his pants, grinding against Charlie in quick rolls of his hips and moaning every time Charlie found a spot that made him shudder with desire.

Charlie's hands were pushing at his waistband, so Jace shoved them away and did it himself, unbuckling his belt and sliding the zipper down in a quick movement. He unbuttoned and shimmied down, his bulge sliding free and straining at his underwear.

Impossible to dissuade, Charlie's hands were back again, this time at the waistband of his underwear, sliding them down carefully.

That left Jace free to do the same to Charlie. He couldn't remember the last time he'd gotten naked so fast, and his head was spinning. Every brush of bare skin on skin, every touch of their hands as they fumbled together, made him breathe out a soft sound of pleasure.

And then... the swollen, flushed skin of their cocks brushed together, the hardened lengths bumping and rubbing as they kicked their jeans off.

Jace's gasp was as sudden and sharp as Charlie's. It took all his focus not to abandon his jeans around his knees and go to town *now*.

He was absolutely high on Charlie in a way he couldn't remember having felt before.

It was terrifying, yet liberating, because everything he did, Charlie didn't just rebuff... he pushed it to the next level. Already, his hand wrapped around their cocks, and *Jesus* that was a good idea.

Jace gasped, then leaned down to suck on Charlie's throat and lick along his jaw, kissing behind his ear. Charlie's scent was strong, and he could hear every little hitch in Charlie's breathing as their cocks rubbed. The hard heads slid across each other, all bumps and veins. Surprisingly strong, Charlie's tight hand wrapped around them...

"Want you to come on me," Charlie whispered, making Jace's whole body flush with heat at the mental image. "Just like this."

"We should... condoms...?" Jace could barely form the sentence.

Charlie huffed out a quick laugh of agreement. "You tested? I am. I'm fine. Or would you rather?"

"Yeah. No, this is..."

"Too good to stop." Charlie's hand was tight, squeezing the base of their shafts now as he slowly thrust up against Jace. "I know, babe. I can't help it either."

"Oh, God." Jace was almost trembling now from how fucking intense it was, and then he made the mistake of looking at Charlie.

Charlie's eyes were fixed on his, his lips wet and slightly parted as he watched Jace's expression. Those gorgeous high cheekbones, the sharp angle of his chin... he was *gorgeous*. Jace couldn't believe he'd gotten this man into bed, let alone so intent on *him*.

What was he looking for? Pleasure? Well, he'd find that in spades. Jace's cheeks were flushed, his eyes half-closed as his skin tingled with electric pleasure.

His nerves were overloaded with all the input: the warmth of Charlie's legs against his inner thighs flooded his, the pounding of their hearts as their chests pressed together, and of course, their cocks.

Fuck. This was *good*. Charlie stroked slowly up and down their shafts, his palm sometimes running over both heads, dragging his fingers along or around the edges of the heads. The most sensitive spots—the underside, right beneath the head—were pressed firmly together, and every slide of skin on skin made him clench with pleasure.

Jace couldn't stop himself—he thrust against Charlie and grinned when Charlie's head rolled back and he groaned in approval. He braced his forearm on the bed next to Charlie's head, mouthing at his jaw as he set himself into a slow, steady rhythm.

Jace let Charlie keep his hand around their cocks for another minute before his hand fell away. Frotting against Charlie's cock and stomach felt unbelievably good, and Jace wanted to leave him sticky, sweaty, and loose with pleasure.

"Yes," Charlie gasped, his nails running sharply down Jace's back. That would leave marks, and Jace loved it. "Just like that. Fuck, *yes...*"

Jace stifled his moan, mouthing Charlie's throat as he thrust. The tiny vibrations against his lips when Charlie's sounds of pleasure spilled freely were the most erotic thing he could imagine.

"Yes, yes, *yes*," Charlie gasped, his body tensing slowly and arching. His thigh muscles shook against Jace's inner legs, his fingertips pressing hard into Jace's back before he grabbed Jace's hips. "Yes, *please*, oh my God, fuck..."

"Noisy little bastard," Jace managed, but his own voice was faint with pleasure. He was so fucking close. The edge was ever closer, his head spinning. As much as he wished he could make it last...

"I'm gonna—" Charlie's voice broke as he rolled his head back, his whole body arching. "*Yes!*"

His cock was shuddering, pulsing against Jace's. Stickiness coated both their shafts, making those last few thrusts deliciously wet and warm and filthy good.

Jace dug his nails into Charlie's hip to hold him down as he thrust against him. Their lips didn't meet, but they were so close Jace could feel Charlie's short, sharp gasps against his lips. Jace's whole body coiled tight, and then he came, slumping against his forearm.

"Oh, *God*, yes!" Jace grunted, heat flooding him so fast and hard it felt like a wildfire was raging through his brain. The spark and fuel were all Charlie.

Everything was Charlie: every thought, every sound and sight and sensation, and every shudder of pleasure was for him.

Only when his cock started to soften did Jace's head clear enough to wrap his brain around that thought.

Holy shit. He'd just had sex, and it was good. No, better than that. Great.

With *Charlie*. And it was *great*.

Like that, Jace's nerves were back. He cautiously eyed Charlie, but Charlie's eyes were closed as he sprawled bonelessly across the bed, one arm over his head, the other hand still on Jace's lower back.

As Jace peeled himself off Charlie just enough to roll onto his side next to him, Charlie stretched languidly and opened his eyes, pointedly looking down at himself. "Fuck."

"You're a mess," Jace pointed out with a low laugh.

"I think that's half your fault. No, more than half," Charlie winked.

Jace's cheeks were already flushed, but his eyes widened as he glanced back down at Charlie's stomach. Surely it hadn't been *that* long.

Charlie's laugh was sudden and rich as he wrapped his arm firmly around his back. "I meant it was your fault we wound up here, but yeah, you had heavier balls than a cannon—"

"Oh, shut *up*," Jace groaned, trying to wrestle Charlie's arm off him as Charlie held tighter.

"Maybe I should call you that. Cannon."

"You're *such* a dick," Jace smacked Charlie's arm away and rolled away from it, which put him firmly on top of Charlie again while they both laughed.

"You love that, too. Apparently as much as my ass," Charlie stuck out his tongue playfully.

Fuck. He was adorable, and Jace felt *good*. But no. This was just the sex talking. A good orgasm made anyone seem bearable.

Jace pushed himself up to his knees, escaping Charlie's playful touches. "I better..."

"Get clean?"

"Yeah."

"Loser. You know where the shower is, baby," Charlie giggled. Oh, yeah. He was strung out of his mind. Again, just the sex talking. "Don't drive."

Jace rolled his eyes and climbed off the bed. He was sober, but he wasn't about to say it. That would mean admitting all of this wasn't just a bad drinking decision. "I'll just get washcloths or something."

"So romantic." Charlie stole a slap of Jace's ass as he walked off.

As he glanced around the small bathroom for cloths, Jace took a quick glance at himself in the mirror. It took him a few seconds to recognize what he was seeing: his own face looking several years younger. He had laugh lines instead of the dark circles under his eyes.

Maybe he'd needed this.

Jace had barely wiped them both clean when Charlie pulled him back onto him, and he didn't have the energy to resist. He laughed—how damn much did Charlie make him laugh? Who last had? Not resisting, Jace tumbled onto him. He didn't *have* to rush off tonight.

Charlie fumbled for the blankets to pull them up to their waist. "Inner or outer?"

"You look like you need a good big spoon," Jace smirked. "If I let you be, you'd be feeling me up all night. C'mere."

"Perfect. In the morning, you can just get started," Charlie murmured, turning onto his side and scooting back into him.

Jace laughed again. Charlie fit perfectly against his chest, the rumble of his voice sending little vibrations through Jace's hand. Which was on Charlie's chest. How did that get there?

But he couldn't pull back, either. He didn't want to. For tonight, he wasn't going to.

Sleep dragged at his mind before he knew it. The last thing he remembered was pressing his face into the back of Charlie's neck while Charlie slid his leg back between his.

No, the last thing he remembered was the feeling.

Warm. Safe. Happy.

8

CHARLIE

Jace was a lot less annoying while asleep, Charlie would grant that.

In fact, sprawled in his bed while Charlie sat on the edge and watched like some damn creepy stalker, Jace looked downright beautiful. Relaxed, for once. It suited him.

He was gorgeous even all wound-up and stressed, but when the subtle stress lines softened and he gave one of those rare genuine, broad smiles, Charlie's heart soared at the sight. Strong jaw, thick brows, the kind of determined, level expression he'd expect from a hero like him...

Charlie didn't usually let them stay the night. He'd let Jace stay. Why?

God. He didn't know.

It wasn't like he'd been drunk. By the end, he'd been sober, and he was almost afraid Jace had been, too. Writing this off as a hate-fuck was both too simple and wrong.

There was something there... chemistry he hadn't been imagining.

Charles stretched slowly and stood, and then Jace shifted in bed.

Shit. He was up.

"You're an annoyingly early riser," Jace murmured, his voice hoarse.

"Ten out of ten. First sentence and you're already being a dick. I'm so proud," Charlie teased, but his spirit was light. "I find you annoying, too."

"Good." Jace covered his mouth and yawned, but maybe he was smiling—his eyes crinkled as he blinked them open. Then he was looking at him.

Their gazes met and they couldn't look away. Jace's light blue eyes were fixed on his, and... fuck. He was even prettier tangled up in his sheets. Charlie's heart was hammering and he didn't know why.

He really had to stop letting guys get to him like this.

"I was worried we had to like each other now," Jace teased, finally looking away and around the room.

Charlie snorted with amusement. "Yeah, right. Nobody can make us do that."

"But we gotta get along for—" Jace covered his mouth with the back of his hand for a yawn again, and it crinkled his forehead adorably. "For the sake of the wedding," he finished.

Charlie groaned. "I know. For the sake of the happy couples."

"That doesn't sound very happy," Jace teased.

Charlie eyed him, but the way he was smiling, it didn't seem like he was annoyed by Charlie's lack of optimism. "Yeah, it's just annoying. All the lovey-dovey couples around."

Jace sat up, pushing the sheets away from himself and rubbing a hand through his hair. "Christ. I know. I mean, it's good to see them happy..."

He got it. Charlie's heart rose with relief, and it was like a dam breaking free. Finally, someone who did. "Yeah, exactly. I'm happy for them, but... it's a lot of pressure. Even the unsaid expectations."

"We don't all need that shit," Jace shook his head. "Everyone keeps wondering when I'll... you know, be ready for another relationship. Like I can't just be happily alone."

"Uh huh. Guys keep getting attached to me," Charlie made a face. "Makes it hard to hook up."

"So you go in saying 'no strings' and they try to tie one on?" Jace grinned. "How terrible. Must be hard having men mooning over you. Is that compliment-fishing?"

Charlie startled even himself with his own laugh. Cheeky bastard, but it distracted him from his morose moment. "Just a statement of fact."

"Charlie: breaker of hearts. Noted," Jace teased.

"Not like Mr. 'I'm not available for a strangely specific number of weeks' is any better, there," Charlie retorted, easing to his feet and padding to the bathroom.

Jace smirked. "You wanna know why that is?"

"Mm." Charlie left the bedroom door open as he crossed the hall to the bathroom, then looked in at Jace again. "Why?"

"I got divorced."

Charlie paused at the sink to grab his razor. He hadn't expected that. He didn't know *why* it was such a surprise... it was kind of obvious, in retrospect. "Oh. From a woman?"

"No. I'm no closet case," Jace smiled. He was following to the bathroom now, rubbing his eyes. "Mind if I—" he nodded at the shower.

"As long as you share."

Jace drew a long, weary sigh. "I'll deal with it, I guess."

"What a ray of sunshine. No wonder you got divorced." Charlie winked at Jace.

Jace looked taken aback for a second. Then, he grinned.

"Nobody has the balls to joke about it like that. *Nice.*" And he wasn't sarcastic—he was actually glowing with pleasure and amusement.

It was a gorgeous look on him, like when he slept.

"Well, it's not like I wanna be nice to you or anything." Charlie let his hand trail down Jace's arm as he moved past him for the shower.

Jace's gaze at him was warm, if momentary. "Of course not."

Good. They were on the same page. And right now, that page might involve getting lucky in the shower.

Shaving could wait.

## 9

## JACE

Jace wasn't allowed in the room, but he watched the broadcast of the inquiry announcement from his living room.

He already knew what was coming. The meeting yesterday had been short, sweet, and to the point.

*Not at fault.*

The phrase—plucked from the prose that had been carefully crafted, so as not to distress the family seeking closure, yet not admit guilt on the department's part—rang around his head.

Whose fault was it, then?

It wasn't the wind's fault, for nobody could hold weather accountable for human deaths in a complex situation like this.

It wasn't Hans's fault. He was new; he hadn't developed his instincts enough to know when to back off, and technical knowledge failed in newbies when conditions were complex.

And it wasn't his fault, apparently. A combination of conditions, less-than-optimal decisions—none so bad as to be indicting, but all stacking up to yield the worst possible outcome: loss of life.

Well, second-worst. Worst would be loss of life for something stupid, like preserving an empty building. That happened sometimes, and it pissed Jace off more than anything.

Hans had died trying to save Sandy, the father of that little girl, Sophie. They hadn't known then that Sandy was past saving. It was a hero's death.

Fuck. Jace's chest was tight again, and he was missing the announcement. He took a few deep breaths.

His boss, the city administrator, finished by thanking the family of Hans, and all the heroes involved that day, for their service and sacrifices. Nice. No political wrangling, but it still left a bitter taste in Jace's mouth.

It was easy to praise heroes, but who would stand by them? It had to be him. He had to have his men's backs, and right now... he wasn't even sure he had his own.

The call came about forty minutes later.

"Jace. It's official. You're back on duty."

If this was what he'd been waiting for, why did it feel like yet another nightmare?

Their conversation was quick and terse. Just as well, because Jace wasn't sure he could hold it together.

A few minutes later, the phone rang again. It was Liam.

"Hey, man. I hear you're back. Welcome back!"

"Thanks. Not officially yet. I will be on Monday. We have to sort out shift scheduling with the interim chief."

Liam sounded enthused. "Good. We've really missed you, Chief."

Bless him. He had no idea how much Jace needed to hear that right now. Jace drew a breath, then smiled at the receiver to soften his voice. "Thanks. It's been weird not being at work."

Something must have been off in his voice, because Liam paused. His voice was a bit different when he spoke again. "You free tonight for a beer?"

Normally, he tried to avoid getting closer to any one of his guys than the rest, so it didn't seem like favoritism when leave picks conflicted. But this wasn't normal.

Honestly, Jace wasn't sure he could pull off tonight alone.

"Yeah. You got plans to talk about?"

"Sure do. I need to know what suit colors will look good on you," Liam joked.

"Anything but black."

"Gotcha. Lime-green it is. Tonight at, oh... seven? I'll text you a place."

Jace tried to keep his voice relaxed. "Perfect. See you then."

Despite spending the evening carefully planning what he'd say, it was way less emotional than Jace had feared. He just showed up, grabbed a beer, and took a table with Liam.

They got to talking about sports first, then Chris's latest pranks at the fire hall. He could tell Liam was altering a few bits so he wouldn't get his best friend in trouble, but Jace would find out the truth sooner or later if it really mattered.

Finally, two beers in, Liam popped the question.

"So, how've you been finding... Charles, isn't it? To work with on all my wedding stuff?"

It was an effective distraction from the events of the day, Jace had to give him that much. Maybe not for the reasons he thought.

*Don't give it away.*

"Um, he's okay. I mean, not to diss your friends' friends or anything..."

Liam raised his hands and laughed. "No, I sensed the air between you guys. Everything okay, though? We haven't, like, thrown you to the wolves?"

*He could eat me up—fuck. No.*

"Um. No. We're just clashing… personalities," Jace decided to put it, carefully. "You know, some people you just don't get along with."

"Uh huh." Liam *seemed* on board, but the tiny smile dancing around his lips could go either way.

"And we push each other's buttons." *Do we ever. Fuck, when he kisses that spot on my neck, uses his tongue to… no. Nope, fuck it, don't.*

Liam dryly murmured, "I noticed."

"But we talked about it. We get on okay. Don't worry about us. We're not gonna ruin the big day by tearing each other's dresses off."

Which put the filthiest thoughts into Jace's head, but he *had* to fucking control them. Jesus. One hookup and he was back on the sex wagon?

Sure, he'd missed it in the month since the divorce, and the several months before then when he and Mike were on the rocks, but… he couldn't throw himself at every single man between here and Monterey.

That made Liam grin. "Good. I'd hate for you to ruin them. He seems like a decent guy, if a bit…" He fluttered a hand slightly.

On instinct, Jace did the decent thing and didn't make his buddy fill in the word—distractible, spacey, woo-woo. "Yeah."

"Yeah. Ash really likes him." It was a guy's way of making up for the harsh comment.

Jace nodded. "I can see that. He's a good man." *Just annoying. And sexy. Fucking hot, and annoying, and laid-back, and probably my opposite in all the best ways, but fucking don't go there. Jesus.*

"He is. And working with him gives you something to do, at least. What about now that you're back on the job?" Liam frowned. "I don't want to overload you, I know your job's got a lot to it..."

"Don't worry, man," Jace assured him, shoving his arm. "I won't let it get to me. I'm not gonna spend thirty hours a week pinning reception photos to my inspiration boards. And I don't know if I'm going straight back to work anyway. Again, transition time."

That stopped him having to admit he wasn't sure he was physically capable of walking into that station on Monday.

Liam laughed and relaxed, raising his beer a little. "All right, all right."

"And the distraction's good," Jace admitted. Time to move on to other subjects. "So, inviting any nice single friends? For Charles. He needs a guy around."

"Does he?" Again, that tiny smile.

Jace nodded. "He's definitely single. I got that much. I mean, so am I now, but..." he trailed off with a meaningful raise of his brows.

Liam looked sympathetic and nodded.

It wasn't a bad idea. If Charles had a man, Jace would be a lot less tempted to strip down and fuck the man every which way on that king-sized bed until they soaked through the blankets with sweat and cum.

Shit. That was a disturbingly detailed fantasy, and his cock was stirring to life. He had to stop thinking about those pretty lips, the wry smile, the witty banter...

No. He wasn't gonna go there. It was too soon. Besides, the moment Charles found out about the divorce and that it wasn't finalized... no guy wanted that baggage, let alone the rest of him.

Jace had a lot of penance to pay before he'd feel good enough for his next try at a relationship. And he wasn't the type to sleep around now that he was strings-free.

Meanwhile, Charlie was his opposite. From the sounds of it, Charlie slept with every guy he could, as long as they didn't get attached to him. It was a recipe for heartbreak, so he was keeping his heart firmly out of it.

And his dick, he mentally added. He adjusted himself under the table as he casually leaned back to finish his beer.

The fantasies were nice, though. They could stay.

10

## CHARLIE

"So, are you feeling nearly ready to take the plunge?"

"God, Charles. Way to put pressure on me," Ash shook his head. But the nervous tension that had lingered around his face the first few times they'd talked about hang-gliding was gone now.

He looked emotionally ready. That was a whole different thing from being physically ready to launch yourself into the air and ride invisible currents of wind for twenty minutes.

Good. Poor guy didn't need any more stress on him.

Charles still remembered how he'd looked when they first met: pale, strung-out on painkillers, but determined. There had been a spark in his eye that worried Charles at first, but it had turned out to be the good kind.

It was easy to mistake the two primal needs: to live, or to escape pain on your own terms.

"I'm just asking. Making sure we're still on for the sixteenth."

Charles had two good reasons for asking: first, he needed to schedule himself, and second, they *all* needed to know for sure when they could plan Ash's proposal.

As Ash's boyfriend, Chris had his own firm ideas about how he wanted to propose. He was set on doing it on the field after hang-gliding. And Charles had to agree... if he were into romance, that would sound pretty romantic to him.

Ash drew a deep breath and nodded. "I'm up for it. That's the date I've told everyone. I've raised about five hundred so far, and that's not counting a few events I have set up."

"Oh, wow. It's cool you're doing this. I respect you for it, man."

"Well, I respect you for helping with Dylan and Liam's wedding," Ash grinned. "They won't let me run around town still. I keep telling them I'm fine now, but... Actually, I'm relieved," he confessed, leaning in. "I'm not really an event planner, and I don't want to be in the spotlight as best man. It's terrifying. Dylan's doing most of the organizing work on my fundraising events. Don't tell them that, of course. I'd help if they wanted..."

"No, no. Won't breathe a word," Charles assured him. He didn't let his expression hint that there might be more to his exclusion from planning than that.

They were tucked into the corner of a coffee shop near State Street. Ash could drive now, so they could go elsewhere, but Ash said he liked it downtown. The life and liveliness, he'd put it. Charles didn't want to discourage that after the autumn he'd had.

There was a moment of silence while they both sipped coffee, and then Ash drew a breath and wrapped his hands around his cup. "So, uh. Feel free not to answer..." Ash began slowly.

Charles thought he recognized where this train of thought was going, but he let it play out.

"You sort of hinted when I first brought it up that, like... the cause meant something to you." Ash left the statement open-ended, so he could choose whether to answer or not. That was thoughtful.

"Yeah. I went through a rough time for... a long time," Charles half-smiled. "I took antidepressants for a while. Finally got tired of trying different ones and went with St. John's Wort and a SAD lamp, every damn day. So far, so good. And therapy."

"No way. Really? I just started my first meds," Ash confided, leaning in. "Just a very low dose. Mostly, I... honestly, I think it was down to my situation."

"Mmmmmhmm," Charles drawled as he nodded hard. He could understand that.

"You, too? Yeah. It sucks. But... now that I'm in school, I've got the best boyfriend ever..."

"Eww. Gag. Gross." Charles sighed.

Ash burst out laughing. "Hey. Don't diss it."

"I've tried it, I'm allowed to diss it. Well, not tried what *you've* tried, but..." Charles playfully smirked. "I don't think Chris would even notice if I slid down his pole. Naked. Carrying free beer."

Ash snorted with laughter and nodded. "He's... he's, um, single-minded in everything he does. It's too intense for some people, but I love it. I love *him*." He was glowing again, his fingers twisted together as he gazed off just past Charles's shoulder.

"Here we go again," Charles groaned.

"Sorry, not sorry." Ash clearly tried to bring himself back to the moment, pinching his own arm before drinking another gulp of coffee. "So, do I need to be looking for single friends?"

"God, no. That's the opposite of what I need. Men keep

throwing themselves..." Charles trailed off, realizing how it sounded. "Not to humble-brag..."

"Well, if you don't want it, you're allowed to bitch about it," Ash told him firmly. Then, he frowned. "Sorry. I mean, whine."

Charles frowned slightly, eyeing Ash. Had he picked that word up somewhere? Or someone had said it about him. That felt more right. It would explain... a lot. "Yeah."

Ash looked down for a second, then cleared his throat, seemingly snapping back into the moment. "So, yeah. I'm glad to meet someone else who's... had issues."

For a moment, Charles watched Ash. He sat straighter and fidgeted less, and even though he looked tired, he smiled more now. His confidence had grown in leaps and bounds over the last month, too.

"You look good," Charles said simply.

Ash gave him a warm, appreciative smile, sipped his coffee, and let silence fall for another minute. Then, he broke the silence. "So, your whole no-boyfriends thing isn't connected to that?"

Charles made a face and laughed. "Wow. Armchair therapist here."

"Sorry! Ignore me if you want," Ash laughed sheepishly. "I just... therapy has been helping me. And now I'm, like, regurgitating things."

"Jesus. So I'm only getting secondhand therapy. Sloppy therapy seconds. Therapy puke. Disgusting, Ash," Charles grinned.

Ash was doubled over the table with laughter. "No! Okay, Jesus. Just ignore me when I do that." He tried to wave Charles off.

Charles beamed. "No, it's more fun to make you go redder than those lilies. Wow. Look at that."

"Ugh." Ash covered his face. "I'm starting to lose my brain-mouth filter. I think I'm around my boyfriend too much."

"It's fine." Charles quelled the flame of annoyance in his chest. *My boyfriend* this and *my boyfriend* that. As much as he liked Ash, people who'd recently gotten together were always like this.

Good thing he'd found one person who agreed with him. Unfortunately, that person was also devastatingly hot and attractive, when he wasn't busy being a prick. He even called him Charlie, and somehow, Charles had found he didn't mind it. If he wasn't careful, he'd start thinking of himself... Wait, had he already?

Ash was talking. Oops. "What?" He blinked.

"I said, *now* you're looking dreamy."

Charles rolled his eyes. "You're imagining things. I'll let you know the moment someone worth more than one night walks into my life, okay?"

Ash laughed, but it was warm. "I'm sure he will."

Charles changed the subject to Ash's physiotherapy, but his mind was still on that week's scorching hot sex, and the conversation the next morning.

He'd never had a relationship quite like this before.

And the scary part was, he liked it.

## 11

## JACE

As he walked into the city hall, Jace adjusted his tie. It felt strange to walk in wearing his admin clothes, but that was the nature of his role.

He was the bridge between the executives—the guys who did the light desk work and didn't understand what really went on further down the food chain, and the guys at the bottom of said food chain who deserved better than they often got.

On the whole, his relationship with the department was pretty good. He hadn't had any major clashes, he got along well with the administrator, and now that the inquiry was complete, his reputation was—apparently—fine.

He'd believe that when he saw it.

"Morning, Ken." He passed by the secretary's desk and slapped it lightly, offering the guy who jolted to life behind it a big grin. "Sleeping on the job?"

"No, man. Just... didn't get my coffee." Ken looked embarrassed as he shuffled papers together. "I wasn't expecting you. Is Sean?"

"Sure. Sure he is." He wasn't, but Jace wasn't going to tell him that. He didn't want the contents of this meeting being made public. He felt bad enough just walking in asking for it, let alone broadcasting that he was doing it.

Jace took another deep breath before his chest could get tight, before his thoughts started to race and spiral out of control into some unimaginable horror that might result from doing this. He was pretending to be cheerful and energetic. He wasn't gonna screw it up now.

"He's just through there, I don't think he's got anything important going on," Ken told him.

"Thanks," Jace nodded, making a mental note to bring in donuts next time. He headed through to Sean's office, already rolling the words around in his head.

"Chief Williams. Pleasure to see you again. So soon?" Even though Sean was technically his boss, he almost always used his honorific title. It was a sign of the respect he had for the job Jace did, and one of the main reasons Jace had stuck to this job like mud.

"Yes, sir. I'd better close the door." As Jace settled into the chair opposite Sean, he straightened up automatically.

Sean didn't seem surprised to see him there. "What can I do for you?"

"It's about the job. Well, technically, about my leave."

"I wondered if we'd have to chat about that," Sean nodded, a frown crossing his face now as he leaned back in his chair. "The inquiry's done now. Has that helped you at all?"

"Yeah." Jace wasn't lying; it *had* helped to hear professionals state that there was little he could have done to anticipate all the factors that had been at play. It was a breakdown in communication, and though that nearly always meant one in leadership, it wasn't entirely his fault, either.

Well, the inquiry had said not his fault at all, but *he* knew he could have done better.

"I believe there's mandated counselling for all your staff. Did you seek it out?"

"Yeah." Jace hesitated, then admitted, "I went. It was helpful. But I'll need a little more time off. Just to get my head wrapped around the inquiry findings, and... test the waters with my guys. And maybe get back to therapy, if HR will let me."

Sean was already flipping open his calendar. "They'll put you in touch with people again. No problem. Do you think your crew will give you a problem?"

"No, no. Not really. But I need that trust to be solid, not even a little in doubt. If someone hesitates at the wrong time... you know?"

"Yeah. Makes sense."

"I'll need to run more training with them and... be visible. Be there all the time, making the small, yet important decisions, so they know they can count on me for the big ones."

Sean gazed at him for a second. "Yeah." For an admin guy, Sean was pretty cool. "So, off for two weeks? And would more counselling help? I'll get HR to get in touch. You can bump it up to twice weekly, get another four sessions."

"That... would help." It was hard for Jace to admit, but it was true. "I should have time to go by all the stations and talk to people. I'll make that work."

"Of course. I'll get your sick leave arranged with HR," Sean told him. "Thanks for coming to me."

Jace nodded slightly. "Glad to." He was indeed glad he had a boss who wasn't going to freak out if he needed time off to process getting one of his youngest guys killed, so he didn't wind up on the floor during an incident.

Yeah, he really needed therapy. Sean was right. Just to admit his anxiety and deal with it would be a big step in the right direction.

"You wanna make the call for the therapist yourself?" Sean's gaze was sympathetic.

"Yep. I'll go do that now." Jace rose to his feet. "Thanks, sir."

"Anytime." Sean watched him to the door, then raised his hand. "Oh, Chief Williams. You might know already, but the Christmas party's on the weekend. Your deputy was filling me in. If you're feeling up to it... could be a good way to test the waters."

"This weekend? That's awfully close."

"Next weekend. Gives you time to find a plus-one," Sean said, but it was a tentative tease, his smile only half-formed.

Sean was pretty smart, too, Jace would give him that. Everyone knew about the divorce, but nobody was saying it in as many words. He'd bet Sean knew it was more of a relief than a sorrow at this point.

"I'll work on it. No promises," Jace laughed. "See you."

He only had one job now: get himself ready to plunge into the fire again as soon as possible. If he didn't get back into the routine, it would be like falling off a horse.

He might be stranded on the trail, never getting back on, while everyone else disappeared into the distance.

1 2

———

CHARLIE

It was never a good day when Jenny called.

Of course, it wasn't her fault. It was just her job. But seeing Pine Grove's name come up on his phone always made Charles's stomach sink with dread.

"Hi, Jenny. It's Charles. What's up?"

"Just a routine call," Jenny said, the greeting she always started unexpected calls with. Well, he assumed always, except in one case, and it seemed like that wasn't the case today.

It settled his nerves, as it was supposed to. "Oh?"

"Your dad's been having a little more trouble walking and balancing lately. I know you've been noticing the memory issues. We were wondering if you have time today to come in for a chat about his health and sit in on his checkup with the doctor."

"That's a great idea," Charles agreed. "I'm free until the evening."

"This afternoon at three?"

"Works for me. Thanks, Jenny. See you then." He had a

tandem at ten and another at one, and that should give him enough time to pack up and drive to the home.

As he hit the "hang up" button and his Bluetooth disconnected, he drummed the steering wheel. It was another gorgeous day—most days were here, it was one of the perks of California seaside life—and he wasn't going to waste it.

"Everything's ready to go." That was Hannah, the peppy short-haired blond college student he'd hired as his assistant. She was constantly full of energy, which was an attractive asset in an assistant whose job it was to set up all the gear required: the glider, which had to be assembled every time; the tow line and motor; even the safety line.

She was interested in becoming an instructor, so they'd worked out a deal: help in exchange for lessons. She was a quick learner, though, and he was pretty sure he'd be out of an assistant within a year.

"Thanks, Hannah. Now to wait for the customer—Ford, that's his name."

"Returning, or new?"

"New. I don't know much about him," Charles admitted. "He booked a couple weeks ago, but that's it."

"Did he sound cute? Ford. Sounds... southern."

Charles laughed. "If he is, he's all yours."

"Oh? Have you met someone?"

Instantly, Charles blushed. It was hard not to think about the encounter with Jace. They hadn't met up again—hadn't had a reason to, until tomorrow, when they met before the bachelor party to make sure everyone got to the club on time and the bar was ready for them.

No reason, except wanting to draw that sincere, gorgeous

little smile again from the stern-faced man. Wanting to see him moaning in pleasure, his forehead beaded with sweat, lips parted as his head rolled back... every muscle in that tanned, toned body clenching and rippling...

*Holy fuck. Not here.*

His fantasies could stay firmly in the shower, where they belonged. The guy was off-limits. His friend's soon-to-be-fiancé's boss, and besides... he had baggage. He'd made that clear by not kissing him.

Was it weird how disappointed he was not to have been kissed? Probably.

"No," he settled on. "But every guy lately wants strings."

"Ahhh." Hannah nodded sympathetically. "They do that. Hopefully this Ford guy is ugly."

"And married."

"And boring."

"And Republican."

"Ouch," Hannah laughed. "You've got me beat. But I've dated some perfectly... well, all right Republicans."

Charles grinned at her. "When bad things happen to good people."

A truck rumbled at the field entrance as Hannah laughed at him. "Keep your mind open, Charles. You never know who could just..." she eyed the truck, "roll into your life."

Charles glanced sideways at her and snorted. "Sure. Named Ford. Driving a beat-up Ford."

What did Jace drive? A Cherokee. Nice and classy, not overstated, rugged enough to get to firegrounds and anywhere else he'd need to go. He was the kind of guy who didn't need to prove himself with a perpetually-empty truck bed.

Shit. Now Charles was comparing unknown and probably uninteresting men with Jace. Shouldn't he compare them with Justin?

"Ford, I take it?" Charles greeted the guy—blond and blue-eyed, handsome and rugged, and shit. Probably Hannah's.

"Yes, sir. Are you Charles?" Oh, that Texan drawl was a nice touch.

"I am," Charles smiled. "Ready to go flying?"

Ford was easy to make conversation with, so Charles chatted for a couple minutes about what to expect, then handed him over. "Hannah here will give you the run-down while I double-check the wind conditions."

He already knew exactly what the wind conditions were, but the way they both brightened up when they looked at each other made him smile.

When he had to interrupt a few minutes later, Hannah took a minute to come back to earth before he let her get at the tow engine.

Gay or straight, Texan cowboy or Californian hippie, the differences disappeared when you were rolling down the field at twenty miles an hour.

In the air, there were only updrafts and currents, clouds and sky. When the heart-pounding liftoff was over, it was pure freedom to soar above the earth, as generations of thinkers had yearned to do.

Charles never felt more alive.

---

"Thanks for coming in, Charles."

Charles greeted Jenny with a smile. It was hard on him to be there, but that didn't mean he had to take it out on her. "Of course. I appreciate you keeping an eye on the situation. Is there anything I should know?"

"No sharp decline in his health. He's stable, relatively speaking."

Charles quirked a smile. "Mentally, yes? Just not on the ground."

"Ah, yes." Jenny laughed lightly. "So far there hasn't been major cause for concern. But, obviously, more falls mean more risk." They walked slowly as they talked, and Charles glanced around.

Although it was spacious and bright here, he couldn't imagine it as an actual life. He'd feel trapped in a day, go crazy in a week. Maybe his dad was trapped enough in his mind that he didn't notice the physical walls closing in on him, but Charles felt guilty every damn day about it.

Not that he had a choice. There was no way he could manage his dad's needs and keep him as safe as the trained staff here could. God, he sometimes wished he really were as irresponsible as he played himself off as.

And the older he grew, the more he started to wonder where *he'd* wind up one day. If he never found a boyfriend, a family... That was a thought he really didn't want to pursue.

"In terms of bone and joint weakness...?" he asked instead.

Jenny nodded. "Exactly. Women are at more risk for osteoporosis and those complications, but men's bones weaken with age, too. So the checkup today is just to make sure everything's all right."

They turned the corner into the main sitting area. It was gorgeous and bright, airy, with a high ceiling and glass wall. A center feature in the living room was a fountain with plants.

Jenny looked carefully at him. "Your dad's been asking about you and Justin today, too. We told him you were coming to see him. We don't know if he fully understands the doctor's appointment, but he can't wait to see you."

Charles winced and looked down. "Yeah. He was fond of Justin."

He'd never discussed it with her as such since a year ago,

when he'd gotten his dad settled in here and told her that he'd broken up with him.

That was an understatement.

"Justin was... an ex?" Jenny ventured.

"Yeah." Charles cleared his throat. "Yeah, he was."

"Have you thought about bringing anyone else... newer... around to meet him?" It was a gentle question, not an accusation, so Charles didn't bristle at it.

"No. I... well, there's been nobody." Charles avoided her sympathetic look by inspecting the pretty name plaques on the doors they passed. He liked the color scheme here. Homey, yet kind of like a high-end hotel, all at once. Very well-designed place. "And if there were, I don't know if they'd want to be called Justin... or if he'd know they weren't..."

"Right. We can sort that out, if it comes to it. Honey," Jenny said quietly, stopping him for a moment with a hand on his arm.

Forced to look at her, he paused, carefully meeting her gaze. "Hm?"

"Don't hold your life back because of this. Don't avoid your own happiness. He'd want that. I'm sure of it."

"He thought *Justin*, of all people, made me happy." Then, Charles snapped his mouth shut. Shit. Where had *that* come from? He was over it... or thought he had been. Maybe not so much.

Jenny eyed him for a few long moments, then patted his shoulder. "So show him someone who really does. He might not remember it, but I'm sure he'll be happy. Just think about it. We see too many children here afraid to be with who they want, or do what they want. Feeling like they have to stay frozen in time because their parents are."

Charles's chest was tight, and tears already pricked the

corners of his eyes. It was a hard fucking conversation to have, but Jenny was doing it without accusation or guilt-tripping.

She was trying to open a door to something else for him, and he appreciated that.

"Thanks," he finally murmured. "If the right guy comes along, we'll see. Work keeps me busy, though."

"Ah, I bet. There's good flying year-round here, isn't there?"

Jenny led him into his dad's room, and try as he might, Charles felt time slow again.

"Hello, boys! Or just you today, Charles?" When Charles hugged him, his dad patted his back awkwardly.

"Just me, Dad. Good to see you," Charles said, sinking into the chair next to his dad's while Jenny went to open a window.

"That's a shame. Tell your lovebird I said hi."

Charles's voice didn't crack as he expected it to when he laughed. "I will."

*It's going to be a long damn afternoon.*

13

JACE

"The tuxes are already sorted out."

"Really? Even the grooms'?" Charlie sounded surprised, but pleased.

"Liam and Chris are taking care of theirs, plus Dylan and Ash's stuff. Ours are all done, too." Jace scrolled down the list on his phone one-handed, a beer in his other hand. It gave him a convenient excuse not to look up at Charlie.

"There's not much more for us to do, then, is there?" Charlie asked. "Bachelor party's on for tomorrow. That's it?"

"Good thing one of us keeps a list."

Charlie laughed. "Sure, fine. Well done on the list. Excellent listing."

"Thanks." Jace scrolled. "Ah, we need to organize gifts for both the grooms. How do we handle that, I wonder?"

"Well, Chris said he doesn't want a registry or anything, Dylan got embarrassed about it and refused, Liam went with Dylan's call, and Ash wouldn't want one even if he did know about it, because he'd see it as charity and get pissed off." Charlie shrugged. "Seems easy."

"Right." Jace laughed. "Okay. I can see all of that, actually." He made a note of that.

"Exactly," Charlie said, grabbing a handful of peanuts. "What else?"

"We need to get their rides sorted out from the reception to their hotel after the wedding. Separate cars, I assume. We'll nail down those details."

Charlie smirked. "What's to nail down?"

*You, if you mess this up.* Jace eyed Charlie and rolled his eyes. "Everything. Now, we have to check with Dylan on the exact timing. If everything's happening simultaneously, we'll each have to take charge of at least one of them... getting them dressed and... huh. Four grooms. How the hell does that work?"

"A lot of lube," Charlie shrugged.

Jace kicked him. "Come on."

"What? You never thought it? Couple hunky firemen, tight —as bros, I wouldn't know about the other way—and their adorable boyfriends...?" Charlie smirked. "I bet people wonder."

"You're the person who wonders. That makes you the perv," Jace informed Charlie, but he was trying not to laugh. He didn't think of Liam and Chris that way, and he didn't really know the other two well enough.

"Oh, loosen up." Charlie grinned and kicked Jace back. "Life's too short."

Jace spotted it before Charlie: someone stumbling past them was losing his balance on the sticky bar floor, his hands flying out for balance. The glass was headed right for Charlie's face.

He smacked the stranger's hand away with one of his own, about to grab Charlie's shoulder and shelter his head with the other hand. Charlie's instincts were keen, though; he ducked into his shoulders, covering his face.

"Please!"

It was one word, almost too soft to hear over the dull roar of the crowd at the bar. But Jace's ears were attuned to fine nuances and crackled, muffled radio speech. He easily caught it slipping from Charlie's lips.

His heart jolted for a second, the blood draining from his face.

The guy he'd pushed sloshed his beer across the floor, sloppily apologized, and kept going. Jace watched him off, then looked back at Charlie.

Charlie was sitting up straight again, a smile around his lips. He looked slightly nervous, though.

*Shit.* Jace would let him keep his pride. "Jesus, people get started early here, don't they?" He grinned, not letting on that he'd heard it. "And on a Thursday."

Instantly, Charlie looked more relaxed. "Yeah. This is a pre-drinking spot. I take it you've been out of the bar scene a while."

"You can say that again." Jace's chest was tight now, but not just from thinking about his own divorce.

The small hints Charlie had dropped were adding up to a question he had no right to ask, but desperately wanted to nonetheless. It made him hold his tongue instead of sassing him back when Charlie made fun of his list before prompting him to continue.

"Nah, we can finish this on the weekend. After the bachelor party. Everything else will be happening closer to the wedding date," Jace told Charlie.

*He might need to get away from his thoughts just as much as I do.*

It was a sobering thought, and one he found himself strangely okay with. If this bantering, strange relationship was helping them both, so much the better.

In the end, Jace stuck around for a second beer and a chat about sports. If they moved in a little as they said goodbye, as if to hug, before catching themselves... neither of them mentioned it. They pulled back instead, fired off a cheap shot or two about each other's dress sense at the bachelor party tomorrow, and went their separate ways.

The house was still and quiet as Jace let himself in, but despite the conversation since then, the annoyance of Charlie pointing out every flaw in his team... his mind was still on that moment earlier in the night.

*Please. Please what? Please don't hit me?*

Jace sighed into the darkness as he stripped his shirt and pants, stumbling into his bed.

"I don't get to ask him," he mumbled. Not that *he* cared about the guy, but... *someone* should. Charlie wasn't that bad, after all.

And he'd see him again tomorrow night, for the party.

Jace already couldn't wait.

## 14

## CHARLIE

"You're fresh meat."

Charlie grinned at the startled, then alarmed expression on Jace's face as Jace turned away from yet another hot young hunk trying to sidle up to him.

"Damn. I knew there was something up."

The bachelor party was in full swing, and the hilarity of having four straight firefighters out with him and Jace, plus Liam and Chris, was not lost on him. He was the only non-firefighter there, and men were *flinging* themselves at the crowd of muscled guys. His stomach already hurt from laughter.

They made such a mixed group. Kevin and Glenn were the oldest and youngest and they were sticking together, unwittingly looking like an adorable May/December couple. Jace was older—compared to gay-old, anyway—as was Charlie. Around Liam and Chris's age were both Billy, one of Liam's old buddies in another district, and Toby, who was apparently one of their new recruits.

Pretty much everyone else knew each other, and though they welcomed him—and the straight guys looked to him for help in how to avoid accidentally picking up men here, which they'd already done several times—he was a little on the outside.

And every guy here was calling him Charlie now, following Jace's lead. Not that he minded, weirdly enough. He'd resisted the nickname because of... well, not just because of *him*.

Moving his thoughts along, it was nice to watch Jace in his element, too. He was slowly unwinding around the other guys, like he'd been expecting more distance from them, but they welcomed him as warmly as any of the others. Being the boss had to be tough that way.

Which also put the kibosh on flirting. No chief of a department like his would want to be seen hitting on a guy like Charlie unless he was serious about it, right? From the snippets of information he'd gathered from the other guys, Jace was pretty damn strait-laced.

Before he got the chance to ask Jace how he felt about being fresh meat, they were interrupted.

"Hey, man. I never got the chance to say." Glenn had pulled away from Kevin and was leaning on the bar by them. "Sorry about things with you and Mike."

Jace didn't even flinch. "Thank you. How are you enjoying this place?"

Charlie almost winced. Jace's response was too practiced. He'd had to say it a lot, he was willing to bet. For someone who kept his private life private... well, that must be hard.

Whoever this Mike guy was, they must have been serious. Not just to have been married, but the way everyone was reacting like he'd lost a life partner. Shit, a long-term relationship, then.

He swigged his beer and listened in on Glenn explaining that the bathroom stall door wasn't on its hinges, biting back his smile.

Jace wasn't letting him get away with that. "I'm sure Charlie would know more about that than me."

Charlie mock-gasped and elbowed Jace. "You dirty bastard. I would never."

"Mmm." Jace raised a brow and smirked. "I apologize for besmirching your pure, undamaged reputation."

Glenn fought back a laugh as he looked between them. "Speaking of old married couples."

*Well, nobody was until just now, but someone's got the divorce on his mind...* Charlie bit back his laugh as Glenn realized what he'd said, then panicked about what to say next.

"Nah. I like my husband docile," Jace winked, saving him.

"No, you don't," Charlie snorted. "That would bore you."

Jace looked startled as he glanced over. "Really? You know me already?"

"Enough to know *that*."

Glenn was gone by the time he looked back over, standing close to Kevin again while he snuck glances around the room.

Charlie leaned in, keeping an ear on the conversation of the hunky guys behind them. "Is Glenn really straight?"

"I wonder, too," Jace admitted. "I suspect we'll know by the end of the night," he winked.

Something was off about him, though. It had been since Glenn mentioned divorce. He'd have said he was just sad, but then Jace kept watching the door, like he was expecting someone. Or like he wanted to use it.

"You all right?"

"Yeah, no, yeah, yeah." Jace waved his beer bottle. "Yeah."

"Well, that's the most believable thing I've ever heard you say."

Jace opened his mouth, then closed it tightly and took a deep breath through his nose. As his barrel chest expanded, it was all Charlie could do not to ogle it through his shirt. Finally, Jace settled on, "Worried about things."

It was the most personal he'd probably been, and Charlie didn't want to push it, but he also wasn't going to let this opportunity go. "Things?"

"Hm," Jace nodded in confirmation and swigged his beer again, then stared down at the counter. He looked paler now, and he couldn't seem to stop drumming his fingers on the beer bottle.

*Ohhh. Shit. He's... panicking? Or anxiety? Something like that. About the divorce? How do I distract him—talk about work?*

"Work will take your mind off them."

That was the wrong thing to say. Jace pulled up a stool and sank onto it, his forearms braced on the counter. The way he looked may have seemed just tipsy to anyone else, like he was getting his bearings, but he'd only had one beer.

Charlie pulled up the stool next to him and scooted close so their knees touched, then rested his hand carefully on Jace's arm. "You gotta breathe, man. Just think about something nice. What do you like to do?"

"A lot of sleeping lately."

"What *would* you do, though? Nature? Sports? Pretentious art shows?"

Jace managed a slight smile. "All of those."

"I got this gorgeous spot for hang-gliding. You know the field tucked in behind that park, right down by the beach? The trail up along the top?" Charlie spoke slowly to let Jace think about where it was.

"Oh. Yes."

"That's where I launch from. The views there for a morning or evening flight, with sunrise or sunset? Gorgeous. Just picture those views." He kept talking for a minute, describing the thermals and the scenery while watching Jace's body slowly uncoil.

At last, Jace smiled slightly. "Yeah." He was breathing steadier now, straightening up. "Sorry. Shit. I don't usually…"

"It's fine," Charlie half-smiled. "Just keep breathing." To help break the thought pattern, he changed the subject completely. "You follow hockey at all? No? Their season just began. I don't really, but one of my cousins does. He was telling me all about that kid who's shooting up to the top. Next Gretzky, they say."

Jace nodded slowly. "Really? Never been to a game. No. I did. Ball hockey. It was different, though… You know much about hockey? Or sports?"

"Not aside from football. But my conversational repertoire is limited," Charlie sighed.

"To, what, two things? Hang-gliding and football?"

Charlie snorted, nudging Jace playfully. "Excuse you. I have a third."

"What is it?"

"Your face."

Jace blinked, then snorted. "*Your face*. Nice. Mature."

"I never claimed to be," Charlie smirked. "Well, I'm probably rated M sometimes, but…"

Jace's grip loosened on his bottle as he laughed under his breath. "Yeah, you are." He was watching Charlie a little differently now.

Respect. That was it. Grudging, perhaps, or surprised. Charlie could understand that; this wasn't their default conversational state.

"I'm… You. Sorry about that moment…" Jace tried to start, glancing around. Charlie did, too, but nobody had noticed their few minutes of tete-a-tete.

Charlie shook his head slightly. "Seriously. It's fine. Didn't you notice?" He flipped his wrist over and pulled his sleeve back slightly to show one of the raised ridges before grabbing his beer again. "I know a thing or two about those moments."

Jace winced, then nodded. "I did see them, but I wasn't gonna... I mean. You don't deserve... you're all right, I guess."

"That's overwhelming praise," Charlie burst out laughing, but he was blushing, too. Fuck. That was practically *I love you*, coming from Jace.

Why were his hands tingly, then? Why was his heart thumping like this? The weight in his stomach lifting?

Oh, man.

"Don't fish for more," Jace warned, half-smiling. "Uh, speaking of... I didn't want to press it, but... last night..."

*Shit. He heard.*

Charlie pressed his lips together hard, and Jace stopped talking. When he glanced over at Jace, the other guy was looking a little away, giving him the chance to decide what to say.

*Hell, I don't care. People probably should know.*

"I let myself get beat up one too many times."

"Fuck." Jace was digging his nails into the bottle now, his shoulders tense. "You didn't *let*... I mean. Jesus. That's... I'm sorry."

"Don't get all weepy on me," Charlie warned, but his throat was tight. "But yeah, that was over a couple years ago. No more Justin."

Jace's head whipped up for a moment as he stared at Charlie, probably processing that it was one guy, not just some random homophobe. That was what most people assumed when they heard he'd gotten beat up.

Charlie hated that moment—the moment where they decided how weak he was for having let it happen.

But Jace just frowned. "Well, if we're oversharing..." He

picked at the label, his voice soft as he looked across the bar. "I've been getting anxiety attacks from work shit. The suspension. I mean. I..." he trailed off, licking his lips and swigging his beer.

Charlie stayed silent to let him talk, but his chest was tight. Jace was talking so much to him. He'd never expected that.

"Hans should have been here tonight."

Charlie knew he should have recognized the name, but he couldn't pull it up. He grimaced. "Sorry. Where is he?"

Jace managed a quick, sharp laugh. "Dead. Because I fucked up."

Then the pieces fell into place. The suspension, the inquiry, the fire that Chris had been caught up in...

"Fuck," Charlie whispered, and this time he couldn't stop himself—his hand slid up Jace's arm to his shoulder. "*Not* your fault, man. I saw the headlines."

"That's what they all say. But it's gotta be somebody's fault."

Charlie hummed, but he decided to let that one go. Fighting with the guy when they were finally talking like buddies, if just for tonight, was a bad idea. "So we both have shit to forget about tonight, huh?"

"Looks like it."

Charlie shrugged carelessly toward the dance floor. "Then we better start working on the fun."

His hand slid down Jace's arm again to his hand, pulling him to his feet.

Jace held on tight to his hand for just a few seconds before loosening his grip. Charlie's heart still pounded as he slipped through the crowd with Jace toward the floor, fingers loosely entwined for just a few more seconds before they let go.

It was probably the most romantic moment they'd had.

The rest of the guys were having fun—a quick check

ensured that. Chris was doing some dumb shit with several shots in his hand, Liam was doubled over with laughter, Glenn was flirting with a guy nearby, and Kevin—the married straight guy—was overseeing everyone like a protective mother hen.

"Pretty cool group of guys," Charlie tried to tell Jace.

"What?"

He leaned in close, and their bodies were pressed together as he spoke into Jace's ear directly. "Pretty. Cool. Guys."

Jace nodded. The music was thumping too loudly to say much else, and all Charlie could think about was what had happened the last time they were here.

And how much he wanted it to happen again.

And how long he'd have to wait before it could.

*He'd never take me home in front of his guys.*

Then Jace's lips were on his neck, his hand on his hip. His grip was firm and confident, and when Charlie pulled back to stare at him, he winked.

Charlie nearly stumbled in surprise. *Or... maybe he would.* He grinned back, finally letting himself do what he'd wanted to all evening: comb his hands back through Jace's hair, slowly over his shoulders and back, to his hips.

"You're all right, too, you know." He spoke loud and slow enough that Jace could interpret it.

"Cheeky bastard." That was easy to lipread, too, and Jace slapped his ass for good measure.

Fuck. He burned from head to toe now as he tried to lose himself in the rhythm of the music streaming around them and the lights streaming over them.

But all he could focus on was the heat of the man in front of him.

He'd wait hours if he had to, but there was only one way this was going to end tonight.

They made it all the way to the end of the bachelor party. They saw Liam and Chris off in taxis, made sure Kevin was safe to drive Toby and Billy, and God only knew where the other two had disappeared. Well, no. Jace seemed to have an idea, but he wasn't telling.

They were alone together again.

"That went well," Jace concluded, leaning on the bar near the door.

"I think we owe ourselves a drink, as excellent best men." Charlie winked at him. "The best men, in fact."

Before he could turn to signal the bartender, though, Jace gripped his wrist. "I can think of a better way to celebrate."

Charlie paused, then leaned slowly and deliberately against the edge of the bar again. "Go on."

"Do I need to spell it out?"

"I'd rather you did that against my..." Charlie trailed off, smirking brightly at Jace.

As he'd expected, Jace flushed and glanced around for a second, as if making sure the inappropriate comment hadn't been overheard. Jesus, he *had* been out of the dating scene a while.

"Lips," Charlie finished.

Jace snorted with laughter. "Uh huh. Not even close to a nice save."

"I know, I know. I suck." Charlie winked. "But you don't mind that, do you?" He couldn't help himself. Normally he might have been a *little* more subtle, but... Jace made him want to grab him and ride him to the ground on the spot. When his hand was on Jace's stomach, he felt a washboard ripple under his shirt. Watching his eyes, he remembered the dark, aggressive lust he'd drawn out not long ago.

Holding himself in check was damn near impossible.

"Shut up and get a cab with me." Jace's eyes glinted with another touch of that firm confidence.

A deep thrill shuddered through Charlie's bones. Having Jace tell him what to do was utterly thrilling. In fact, he was getting hard. "What if I want to play hard-to-get?" he whispered, leaning in closer to Jace.

Jace's hand curled around the back of his neck, then flattened against his shoulder blades as he stepped closer. "That's the last thing you are, Charlie." His voice was surprisingly affectionate. "In any way."

And he was right, damn it. Not just in calling him easy, but in telling him he wore his heart on his sleeve.

"I wouldn't want it any other way," Charlie said simply, then pulled away to head for the door.

Jace's hand was still lingering on his back. If he didn't know any better, Charlie would call it a caring touch steering him toward the street. He let Jace handle getting the taxi, too.

"My place?" Charlie suggested. "Or do you want to take turns?"

A smile flickered across Jace's face. "Yours is fine." The way he spoke stopped Charlie from having any second thoughts on his decision.

*He's a natural leader.* And Charlie wasn't exactly a born follower, but he was willing to let Jace take that role. Somehow, it seemed like he needed it.

They were crushed up against his front door within minutes, Charlie losing his breath from laughter as Jace tickled him from behind again and tried to cover his pockets.

"Asshole."

"Cocktease."

"Bastard." He almost closed his fingers around his keys in his pocket, and then Jace's hand slipped under his shirt, his fingers dancing lightly over his stomach. Charlie yelped and stumbled against the door, dropping his keys. "Double bastard."

"All the way," Jace agreed, but he grinned and stepped back one pace.

If his front porch weren't sheltered by this hedge, Charlie was willing to bet Jace wouldn't have been so bold. As it was, the distance Jace had backed off was just enough to let him bend over for the keys, but it could quickly become indecent even for him.

"You are *way* more of a perv than you want to let on," Charlie accused Jace. He stooped for the keys, then straightened up and glanced behind him. He'd fully expected to be ground against, groped, or just eyed up and down.

Instead, Jace just winked. He had his arms folded in such a way that the arms of his goddamn t-shirt showed off his biceps. Fuck. Charlie had been about to say something, but the wall of muscle waiting for him to get inside and climb it completely killed his train of thought.

Charlie managed to unlock the door at last and they both stepped inside. He kicked it shut and kicked off his shoes. "You just like making me squirm."

"It's a great pleasure." Jace's voice was husky and sultry, dripping with intent. Their dislike for each other was a game where everyone won. This was the prize for them to share.

Charlie was hard again. "Take me to bed. Now."

Jace shoved him through the doorway of his room and onto his bed, his eyes almost ripping off Charlie's clothes before his hands got to work at it. He wasn't moving in his usual slow, controlled, careful mannerisms.

This was animal lust, and Charlie fucking loved it.

Charlie raised his arms and wrestled his t-shirt off them while Jace skipped ahead to his belt and jeans. He gasped at the hot hand running over his bare stomach to the belt buckle, trying not to grind into Jace's hand.

It was a futile effort. The moment his jeans were around his knees, Jace's hand slid over the bulge in his underwear, cupping the shaft and applying firm pressure with the heel of his hand from base to tip.

Charlie rolled his head back and cried out with pleasure, twisting his fingers hard in the sheets. There was no other way to verbalize how fucking incredible it felt to let go and let Jace have him.

Any damn way he wanted.

But Jace pulled his hand back, his eyes glinting teasingly as he knelt back to strip off.

Charlie couldn't bring himself to complain, squirming under Jace to kick his jeans the rest of the way off while trying not to tear his eyes off the magnificent sight of fabric lifting away from the pure muscle of his body.

Did Jace even know how fucking hot he was? Like, holy shit. By the time his jeans and underwear were off, he was twisting to pull everything off his ankles, Charlie's gaze was busy wandering up and down the thick shaft that had so perfectly nestled against his own last time they fucked.

"Fuck my mouth," Charlie whispered. "Or let me suck you. I really want to." He licked his lips, only looking up when he felt Jace's stare on him.

Jace swallowed hard, then jerked his head in a quick nod and eased himself back to sit against the headboard. "I don't have condoms."

"I do. When did you last get tested?"

"Since I..." Jace trailed off, his brow furrowing. "A month before we, uh. Did stuff. Last week."

"You haven't been with anyone else?"

"If you want to take that as a compliment, go ahead," Jace rolled his eyes. "Nobody else."

Charlie grinned broadly. He pressed his lips against Jace's shoulder and swung a leg over him to straddle him. "I will, then. I've been using condoms with everyone else."

"Except me last week. Tsch."

"Yes. Fuck off." Charlie slapped Jace's chest, then scooted down to press his lips against the spot. "I don't usually... yeah."

"But you want to skip condoms with me? Again?" Jace cupped Charlie's cheek, his thumb brushing his cheekbone. "Some kind of trust game?"

"Yeah. Suppose." It was more about convenience, and wanting them both locked together and sticky, but maybe there was that, too. Charlie didn't make exceptions. But Jace was telling the truth—it was easy to read. He'd been married for too long, divorced now, not sleeping with anyone else.

"Dumbass."

"Dunno why," Charlie weakly snorted, but his heart was pounding like some grain of truth was trying to push its way through to the front of his mind. "I am, apparently. When it comes to you. Takes one to fuck one, right?"

The words had spilled out without thought, and his already-pounding heart skipped a beat, leaving him out of breath. The moment between them was almost painful as Charlie gazed up the muscled plane of Jace's chest, that palm hot against his jaw, not daring to move or look away. He couldn't tell what was going through Jace's mind, and he could barely tell what was going through his own.

Well, no. Maybe he could. But he was afraid to stop and try.

Jace's hand ran down to his shoulder, then cupped the back of his neck again. He deadpanned, "That's the most romantic thing anyone's ever said to me."

Romantic. It *was*. Oh, fuck. Charlie tried not to let his panic show.

"Unprotected isn't more romantic, though," Jace told him, smirking like he was giving a sex ed class. "It's almost a boner-killer for me."

"Oh. Sorry." Well, that effectively broke the moment.

"Not this time, luckily."

Charlie groaned and nodded abruptly, glad that Jace agreed with him on the subject but resisting the urge to bite him over his tone. "Yeah, your boner's going pretty strong there. I better look close-up. Get a good taste. Just to be sure."

"Then stop talking about it and get to it," Jace told him, grinning cheekily at him.

"Now who's romantic?" Charlie muttered, kissing his stomach.

He *loved* sucking cock and swallowing, loved feeling men squirm under him with need, loved tempting them into fucking his mouth until they slid down his throat. Without a condom? Extra tasty, and tingly hot. It had been so fucking long since he'd had a boyfriend—or anyone he trusted enough to do this.

But Jace was straight-up about everything, and for all he'd called Charlie a dumbass, it was equally out of character for everything he knew about Jace.

So, something about Charlie made Jace lose control just as much as Charlie lost control for Jace.

Charlie revelled in the moment. He took his time to tease the hipbones, every one of that eight-pack, and the lines running between them. By the time he was kissing over the dark fur, Jace's controlling gaze and hold on him had ebbed.

Jace was thrusting lightly, needily, up into the air, but let Charlie take his time kissing from the base of the shaft to the tip.

By the time Charlie wrapped his mouth around the velvety

smooth head, lips sealing around the ridged, swollen skin, Jace was breathing hard, deep gasps.

"Mm," Charlie moaned his appreciation for the salty taste that made his palate tingle.

"Jesus Christ. Oh, God, that's good." Jace's words came in a soft, hoarse moan.

Charlie slid his lips slowly to the base of Jace's cock. His gag reflex was long trained out of him by now, and the look on Jace's face when he slid his lips almost off his cock so he could look up again was totally worth it.

"Holy *fuck*." Jace tangled his fingers in Charlie's hair, and Charlie knew he had him.

"I wasn't kidding when I said to fuck my mouth." Charlie whispered across the tip, then let his tongue trail around the head in slow, sweeping circles.

"Noted." Jace was trying to keep his voice steady, but he whimpered under his breath when Charlie let his tongue linger against the spot where the head joined the shaft. "Oh, fuck. Please."

*That's the magic word.* Charlie eagerly pushed down onto his cock again, drawing the shaft across his tongue and playing Jace like a fiddle.

Jace thought he was easy? Jace was the easy one. He was writhing, moaning, within a minute. Twitching within two. Groaning Charlie's name like he was on the edge of coming in three.

"I'm—baby, oh my God. I'm so. Fuck. It's. Wow." Jace was gasping words between breaths.

It struck Charlie that the man probably hadn't had a good blowjob in months, if ever. He ran his hand up Jace's chest to tweak a nipple, then pulled back as Jace reached down to stroke his shaft for the last few seconds.

Charlie rested the tip of his tongue on his lower lip and

gazed up at Jace with every ounce of the lust he felt for the up-close sight of that strong hand working the shaft fast and hard, Jace's chest heaving, his groans spilling out freely...

He was hard and throbbing in his underwear, but with his finger running around Jace's nipple and his other hand squeezing Jace's thigh, tickling his balls, he had no hands free for himself yet.

Jace came hard and fast. Charlie lapped at the head of his cock with his tongue, the thick warmth that coated his tongue lightly sweet. Good diet; good man. The pleasure etched on Jace's face was a little painful to watch: disbelief, arousal, and that rare unrestrained joy.

Charlie bobbed his head slowly once more down the shaft and back up as Jace softened, swallowing him clean. When he pulled back and winked at Jace, Jace burst out laughing.

Holy fuck, that was a gorgeous sound. The warmth echoing around the room, the way it filled his expression and hummed through his body...

"What?" Charlie grinned, pulling his mind *off* the too-close-to-romantic thoughts.

Jace shook his head slowly. "I've never..."

"You can't tell me you've never had a guy blow you like that," Charlie teased, though pride was starting to glow in his chest. He'd heard that before, actually. More than once. He took damn pride in his talents.

"Then I don't know what to tell you. Take the damn compliment," Jace ordered.

Charlie smirked. "Fine. Bossy."

Jace hesitated for a second, then grabbed Charlie by the shoulders and pushed him onto his back.

"You don't need to," Charlie told him in an undertone. Sure, he *wanted* Jace to blow him, but he had to give him an out if he didn't like it.

Jace glanced up at him, those dark eyes intense. Hungry. "Do you want it?"

Charlie's whole body throbbed with desire under that look. "Yes."

"Then shut up and let me make you feel good." There was some emotion thickening his voice, and Charlie didn't dare guess what it was.

Charlie relaxed into the bed, melting under Jace's firm hands. He smiled up at the fire chief and murmured, "Okay."

He was in safe hands. In more than one way, any time now.

Jace's hands ran down his hips, thumbs hooking into his waistband as he carefully pulled his underwear down.

"God, about fucking time," Charlie moaned, and there was a deep chuckle from Jace. He cracked his eyes open to enjoy the sight as well as the feelings of the other man braced over him. Naked skin on skin was almost overwhelming, but the warm lips pressing against his neck made him melt even more.

"Yes," Charlie breathed out, his fingers curling into Jace's shoulders as he pushed up against his solid body. It was like shoving a brick wall, and very effective to grind against the rippled abs. God, he could get used to *that* texture...

Jace grinned and nipped his neck. "Bad," he scolded. "Not waiting a second, are we?"

"I had to wait so long," Charlie moaned.

"I thought I came awfully fast," Jace snorted.

"Well, if you wanna insult yourself, go ahead. That way, I don't even need to—ahh!" Jace was sucking hard on his neck. Holy *shit*, that would leave a mark, and he loved it. His whole body throbbed with pleasure at the bite and pull of suction on delicate skin.

He was panting for breath by the time Jace pulled away. "Hm?" Jace teased. "What was that?"

Charlie couldn't even think straight with how much he

ached to feel that wet warmth around his cock. "Forgot. Please. Jace... please."

Jace hissed appreciatively, then kissed down his chest to his nipples. "In a moment."

"Oh my God, you're going to—" Charlie broke off again at the heat and the firm tongue pressing against, then swirling around, his nipple. "Jesus!" His cock twitched, his thighs trembled, his balls drew tight.

He was *not* going to come from heavy petting. What the fuck?

But his body was on edge, his nerves crying for more. Every touch by Jace satisfied every fucking inch of him. His kisses to his shoulder might as well have been his stomach—to his nipple could have been his cock.

*I knew something was up the second I saw him.*

Charlie wasn't letting himself think anything more... extreme... than that. Too early. Way too early.

"Please, Jace, please please," he gasped for breath, "please please—yes!"

Jace's hand gently cupped his balls, then ran up his shaft. Even that much pressure was enough to make him tremble with need and desire. "You're so sensitive," he whispered. That tone was... awed?

Opening his eyes for a quick peek at Jace made Charlie blush from head to chest, heat rushing through his frame. His heart was already hammering against his chest, but his toes curled into the bed with embarrassment and... a thrill.

Jace was looking at him in a way that he couldn't remember anyone doing. If they had, it had been a long time ago.

Charlie lost track of what he was going to even answer, but it didn't matter. Jace's lips were on his stomach now, his finger still circling the skin around one damp nipple.

Jace drew his finger slowly down the middle of his stomach

while he kept kissing ahead of it, all the way down to Charlie's inner thigh.

The hot mouth against the underside of his shaft made Charlie flinch with his whole body again. His nerves screamed for a break, or release, or *something* other than this tease. The tip of his tongue tracing up along the veins of his shaft was just fucking unbearable, but in the best way he could imagine.

Jace dragged his tongue slowly around the head, then wrapped his lips around the shaft and pressed slowly down.

Perfect. Fucking, unbelievably, insanely *perfect*.

Charlie was losing his grasp on time, language, even himself. For the moment, he existed only in the hot contact between their bodies, and the way Jace was taking him into his mouth with such tender attention.

He came hard, pushing the back of his head into the pillow as he gasped Jace's name. He didn't usually do that. He tried not to, because mixing up names was too easy.

Not Jace, though. His name was unique. His alone.

Charlie's chest was tight and warm even as his body settled back into the mattress, and he kept his eyes closed while he caught his breath and shut his brain up. It was just the hormones talking. Endorphins. Whatever.

"I should get going," Jace murmured after a minute, rolling off Charlie.

Charlie finally cracked open his eyes for a look at the other man, but he was avoiding eye contact as he got off the bed.

Just as well. Charlie didn't need any more enticement to say something stupid like *I like you*. To become one of the guys he ditched at a moment's notice.

"Yeah. Long day tomorrow?"

"Oh, yeah." Jace nodded abruptly as he stepped into his underwear and jeans. "You can say that again."

"Good luck with it. If you need anything..." Charlie trailed off.

Jace raised his brow, a smile playing around his lips. "I know my mouth's talented, but seriously?"

"If you need anything, fuck off, I'm busy with tandems from sunrise to sunset," Charlie retorted, grinning back at him.

"That's better."

Charlie walked him to the door when the taxi honked. His fingertips itched to take Jace's hand, to try to preserve this peace between them for a minute or two longer. He wished he had pockets to slide his hands into. Instead, he had to fold his arms as he leaned against the wall by the front door, watching Jace get his shoes on.

"That was a good bachelor party."

"Yeah."

Jace paused, then turned to face him and held out a fist.

Before he could think twice, Charlie flinched at the hand coming toward him, even if it was lower than he expected. Then, his cheeks burned with embarrassment.

Jace didn't react, though, just held his fist there until Charlie raised his own and fist bumped him.

"Good job, team," Jace said simply and winked. "Now to ace the proposal."

"For as unromantic as we are, we make pretty damn good best men," Charlie agreed. "Catch you later."

"See you, Charlie."

Despite the carefree tone between them, Charlie found himself hovering near the front door, leaning around the edge to watch him into the cab safely before he closed the door.

He was supposed to be relieved they wouldn't have much to do together for the next few weeks, not... disappointed? Was he actually *sad* he wasn't going to get to push Jace's buttons until then?

Charlie groaned, long and low, and leaned against the front door. His voice echoed in the empty hallway, but he spoke up anyway, as if someone would appear from nowhere and make sense of this fucked-up... thing.

"What the hell is wrong with me?"

15

————

JACE

"What the hell is wrong with me?"

Jace said it in a mutter under his breath after a quick check of his surroundings. Nobody within half a block. He might be in therapy, but he wasn't going to be the crazy guy walking around talking to himself.

If he were really honest with himself, he knew exactly what was wrong with it. He and the therapist had been over it extensively.

All strictly work-related. He'd kept Mike off the table. That was another issue altogether, and his fire department psych didn't need to know the finer points behind his divorce. When she'd tried to mention it, he had politely overridden it.

"Morning," he muttered to someone who passed, waiting until they and their shopping bags were out of his way before he headed for the car.

Fuck, he still had to go Christmas shopping for his own family. It wasn't like him to put that off, but this year... everything felt different.

For Mike's faults, for his impulsiveness and his secrecy and his dishonesty, he'd also been a grounding influence in Jace's life. Odd to think about since he'd caused Jace more gray hairs than anyone else, and he'd made it clear his settling down was only reluctant. As it turned out, a pretense, not just a reluctant act.

But having him around had made Jace careful of everything. Careful not to leave him alone for too many days in a row, careful to read his moods right, careful to show affection in all the small ways he could, careful not to overstep those boundaries in public around his less tolerant subordinates.

Careful was so fucking exhausting, though. And for all the good *careful* had done him that evening a few months ago, it could fuck off.

Jace was in a bad mood as he dropped into his car seat and slammed the door shut, then glanced at the meter. Still a couple minutes left. Good. He didn't like driving in any state that could distract him from safety.

He pulled out his phone, intending to search for kitten photos or something to distract himself.

Instead, he had his phone out and was calling Charlie.

*What? Why him?*

"Hey, big J."

Despite himself, Jace cracked a grin. "That's a terrible nickname. Never use it again."

"Sure, Cannon. What's good?"

He sounded even more... *chill* with his lingo than he was normally. Unless he toned it down for Jace's sake, which was an amusing thought.

"Uh. I. You know." Jace didn't even have an excuse invented, and his cheeks flushed. "Just seeing if you were telling the truth."

"Uh huh? About my day full of tandeming?"

"Yeah. You don't sound very high up."

"I'm a few hundred feet up."

"What?" Jace yelped. "You should focus—"

"I think the atmosphere's too thin up here for sarcasm." Charlie was laughing under his breath.

Jace snorted as he relaxed. "Asshole. So, no tandem?"

"Just in between now," Charlie assured him. "I've got my assistant double-checking the glider between flights. Eating a sandwich. Measuring the wind speed over the cliffs. It's thrills all the time over here."

Jace laughed under his breath. "Makes me want to try it. Occasionally. Then I come to my senses."

"Really?"

"Isn't that atmosphere thin?"

"Ohhh. You're no fun," Charlie groaned. "I thought you were serious. I want to take you."

Jace smirked. "Oh, you're versatile? We can talk about that bridge when we cross it."

"I—you're terrible," Charlie accused him, but his grin was easy to hear. "And if I said yes?"

"I'd say I don't need to know that," Jace snorted. "We're clearly... not doing anything of the kind. Obviously. Once is once."

"And twice is twice. Yeah. We don't get along and all," Charlie snickered. "Sure, man."

Jace hadn't stopped smiling since hearing Charlie's voice for the first time. He was leaning back in his seat now, watching passersby. "Getting along would make life boring. I think we do well considering we don't."

"Mmm." Charlie's voice was playful. "I think I see my next client. He's supposed to be an Aussie."

"Supposed to be? Is he not sure?"

"Shut up," Charlie sighed. "That's what my assistant told me he was."

Jace smirked. "Are you having him over? Gonna take a last-minute shower?"

"There's an idea. Jealous? I'll send you photos."

*Photos of him in the shower?* Jace's brain stalled out for a second. Then, it sputtered back into gear. *Oh! Dumbass. Photos of the Aussie.* "Of your guy? The guy?"

"You're just sad you're not rescuing hot, studly young men from fires."

"It's true," Jace agreed. "Go on, then. Try not to crash."

"Go on, try not to fuck yourself," Charlie laughed. "Bye, b—buddy."

His brief stutter caught Jace's attention, but not for long. He had to focus on driving, after all. Jace hung up and pulled away from the curb before his meter ran out.

He was most of the way home before Charlie sent his first photo: a patch of flowers.

Jace looked around for something to reciprocate with, sitting in his driveway and slowly unbuckling. He finally chose one of the trees in the front yard. He added, *Since we're doing nature?*

Charlie didn't miss a beat. *I like doing it in nature.*

"Oh, fuck," Jace muttered under his breath, climbing out of his car and striding for the house. He waited until he was inside to answer.

*Nudist?*

*Far from it.* Charlie sent back a selfie of himself in what looked like khakis and a neat polo shirt with his gliding company logo. Actually, he looked damn good.

Jace choked back a laugh. *Come to think of it, your sport wouldn't be great in the nude.*

The *hahaha* he got back from Charlie made him grin. Then, Charlie answered, *Why? What are you wearing?* ;)

Jace snorted at the implication. Like they were about to

sext. He sent back a photo: just trousers and a t-shirt with a light sweater. The first three things to hand from his closet. He hadn't especially wanted to leave the house this morning.

*Infiltrating a sports bar?*

He frowned. *What?*

*You dressed like a straight man this morning.*

Jace sent a photo of himself flipping the middle finger, biting back his smile until he took the photo.

Charlie sent a photo of himself sticking out his tongue at the camera, crossing his eyes.

He looked... adorable. Jace hesitated, fingers hovering over the keyboard as he crashed on the couch, trying to figure out what to say.

*Attractive face there. This is why you're single. :) Doing anything tonight?*

The second he sent it, he doubted himself. It was one thing making those jokes in person, but it was quite another in text.

And there was the minor fact that some part of him had actually meant that as an invitation, not just taking the piss out of him.

And he didn't get a response. One minute turned to five, then ten. And it was only fifteen minutes in that Jace realized it had been about the top of the hour when he'd texted.

He probably wasn't pissed off—or he was, but either way, Jace had to wait until the tandem session was over.

He groaned and collapsed on the sofa, covering his face with the pillow. Sending another text now would look lame: either he'd look desperate for a date if he clarified he'd meant it, or he'd look like he was backing off and had meant it if he clarified it was a joke.

Plus, he wasn't sure which direction he wanted that card to fall.

Just as he was drifting off, the phone vibrated against his chest, making him just about jolt out of his skin.

*Nope. I'm yours.*

A big grin spread across Jace's face. He answered in a word: *Sushi?*

Charlie's response was instant. *Can't wait.*

---

"You've gotta be joking."

Jace grinned at Charlie, then nodded at the sushi restaurant. "What?"

"This is the place that does, like, live flame. Wouldn't you hate it?" Charlie was leaning on the wall near the restaurant entrance, but he pushed himself upright as Jace approached.

"So I know they've been inspected to recent safety standards," Jace retorted, his eyes flickering appreciatively up and down Charlie's body.

Charlie seemed utterly unaware of how attractive he was in that lean, lanky, *tall drink of tasty Californian surfer dude* way. He'd gone with a proper button-down shirt and trousers, and his belt matched his shoes.

Muscled in just the right places, slender in the rest... rounded in the one place it mattered. Jace got a quick look at his ass as he turned for the door, too.

"You look good today," Charlie told Jace as he pulled the door open for him. "I hope you didn't dress up for me."

"Oh, I would never," Jace assured him, deadpan. "Nor you me, right?"

"I just dressed like this in case the cops pulled me over. Or the firemen had to come save me from the restaurant fire."

"Oh, ye of little faith." Jace knocked on the doorframe as they passed through, then gave his surname for the reservation.

They settled down at the small table near the bar, both of them instinctively looking toward the grill in the middle of the place.

It was a sweet little place here, and exactly right for a date. Jace was almost sweating at the obvious question hanging between them.

"God, this street is full of... hipsters and happy couples. You have terrible taste," Charlie informed him.

Jace rolled his head back and laughed. "Don't sweet-talk me."

"I hope you know me better than *that* by now," Charlie told him, and when Jace looked at him again, he winked.

"I'm beginning to," Jace told him seriously. He was met with a few seconds of silence, and his cheeks flushed slowly. He glanced around for help, and the only thing to save him was the grill. "What are they cooking?"

"I don't know." Charlie's voice was breathless, but he cleared his throat and repeated himself firmly. "We can ask."

"Oh, no, I can see. Chicken."

"Chicken teriyaki or something?"

Jace nodded briskly. "Yeah. That's about right."

They didn't make eye contact for a few more moments, both busily flipping through their menu. They ordered drinks and kept staring at the menus for a few moments.

"My boss mentioned a Christmas party this weekend," Jace finally said, when the silence was too painful.

Charlie perked up. "Ooh. I love parties."

"That makes one of us."

"What?" Charlie gasped. "You don't like—think of all the potential. Drunk coworkers, embarrassing gift swaps. That shit sounds great. I don't get office Christmas parties."

That was a good point, actually. Jace hadn't thought of it. "Oh. Well, want to trade?"

"I come to yours, you come to mine?" Charlie grinned. "Sounds like what we're doing now."

*Oh my God. Innuendo. Again.* Charlie couldn't goddamn help himself, and Jace wanted so badly to point that out.

But Charlie barely stopped to catch his breath before he grew flustered and talked on, not giving Jace the chance. "Anyway, ha ha. Yeah. I'll come to yours. If you want me to. I wouldn't be in the way?"

Jace shook his head. "The opposite. People might stop treating me like the sad divorced guy. I won't get hit on by the office ladies trying to make me feel better."

"Ouch," Charlie winced and laughed. "Okay, I'll come, then. Remind me never to get divorced. Oh. Or married, I guess. That would solve that problem."

Jace flipped the menu shut, stretching his arm along the edge of the table and leaning in. "You don't want to?" It was in keeping with what Charlie had said before, but Jace could also see the romantic edge to Charlie that he tried to keep hidden.

"I'm not dying to," Charlie answered casually, but he was staring intently at his menu again. "But, you know. Whatever happens, happens. I'm not *anti*-anything. I'm not leading the picket line..."

Jace could have kissed the waitress for coming back to take their food orders. What the hell was up with this? They hadn't made fun of each other once.

When the waitress brought back appetizers, she also brought a lit tea light holder and placed it between them, next to the flower vase, before winking at them conspiratorially.

Jace couldn't look at Charlie again. His cheeks burned too hard. "Shut up."

"You brought me on a *date*," Charlie smirked. "How misguided."

"It's not my fault we look like a couple." Oh, fuck. Oh, no, Jace was going to put his foot in it if he weren't very careful.

Luckily, Charlie laughed and nodded. "One weird couple we'd be."

"The ones fighting in the corner over stupid little shit and then making out on the porch afterward? Yeah, that couple," Jace laughed quietly.

He wished he could find the courage to tell Charlie that that didn't sound like such a bad thing. In fact, maybe it was exactly what he needed.

But he stayed silent, and Charlie laughed, too, and finally—finally!—changed the subject to something safe. A little sports talk again. Jace could get on board with that if it would stop him from hitting on Charlie quite so much.

It was easy to make fun of Charlie's football team, and even though neither of them really followed sports, it gave them something to dig at each other about that wasn't... themselves.

*It's never going to happen. You don't even want it to! Stop rebounding and enjoy his friendship.*

Just friends. That was all he wanted.

1 6

CHARLIE

"What was I thinking?" Charlie groaned. He pulled at his tie, hooking his finger into the collar to pull it away from his neck, then ran his hand over his hair.

He felt like his personality was being squeezed, pinched at the corners in order to fit into these nice clothes. It was only a dark button-down shirt, white pullover sweater, and dark navy slacks, but the polished belt and pinching shoes were too weird.

Charlie was going to spend the night on the arm of this guy he'd started off hating, and now he... hell, he was thinking of himself as Jace's annoying nickname for him.

*Charlie* had been how the kids teased him, or Justin... fucking Justin. He had to get his brain off Justin. Jace was *not* Justin, nor would he ever be.

But people would think they were together. And were they? They'd stopped making fun of each other, except to lighten the mood. When they did, it was *way* more fun than being sweet and doting on each other. Hell, they were dancing around serious conversations together. And they'd fucked, more than once.

It was all leading them down a path he wasn't sure he wanted to think about.

The knock on the door came at exactly seven, just as Jace had promised. Charlie bit back his smile. "Come in!" he shouted as he flicked off the bathroom light.

Jace pushed the front door open and stuck his head in the hallway. "Any half-naked men hanging around? Oh. It's just you."

"I told them to wait in the bedroom until later." Charlie blew Jace a kiss as he grabbed his coat, then patted down his pockets.

Jace eyed him carefully and let the front door close, stepping into the front hall. Before he could pull Charlie in by the tie, Charlie held out a hand, then wagged a finger. "No touching the hair."

"Got it."

"Or wrinkling my pants."

"Mmhmm."

Charlie's fingertip pressed against the broad barrel of Jace's chest. The sleek, merino wool sweater he wore flattered the curves of his muscles perfectly. It distracted him from the other ultimatums he was preparing.

Jace took his chance to grab Charlie's hand and yank him in by the wrist until he stumbled against the fireman's chest. Then, Jace wrapped his arm around Charlie's waist and pressed one slow, sweet kiss against his lips before tangling a hand thoroughly in his hair.

"Bastard," Charlie complained in a mumble against those warm lips, but the heat and firm support of Jace's body against his was much too good to turn down.

At last, a kiss. Easy as anything, casual, not made to be a big deal. Just the way he needed it. And Jace tasted sweet but smelled minty, fresh and bright-eyed and ready for the office party.

"Are you complaining?" Jace murmured, letting go of him and pulling back a few inches.

Charlie almost stumbled forward but grabbed Jace by the front of his sweater. "Don't you fucking think about it. Kiss me again. Now." When Jace smirked but didn't move, he glared. "Kiss me, before I..."

"Make me?" Jace challenged, tilting his chin up slightly. "I'd love to see that, shorty."

Charlie wasn't much shorter than Jace, but a couple inches and the right head angle made all the difference. He narrowed his eyes, then looped both arms around Jace's shoulders and hoisted himself up. It was a pull-up of sorts against Jace's body. He locked his legs around Jace's waist as soon as their crotches ground together, Jace's hands automatically coming up to cup his ass.

"Jesus!" Jace exclaimed, bracing himself to catch Charlie's weight. Charlie sure as hell felt him squeeze, too.

Charlie nipped Jace's neck, then leaned back just enough to take in his expression. "You told me to."

"So I say jump, and you..."

Charlie flipped him off, then realized his arm was behind his head and he couldn't twist it around the right way without letting go of him. "Fuck off." He kissed Jace hard.

This time, they stumbled against the wall, Charlie's knee bouncing off it as Jace leaned there heavily. Their breathing was heavy, their bodies pressed so tightly together along Charlie's whole body from head to toe. Every little breath he could suck into his mouth, every time he teased the tip of Jace's tongue, a shiver of heat went through him.

And he felt Jace's dick responding. He ground slowly, his head spinning. He couldn't remember what was so important that Jace was here—all that had been forgotten the moment he caught a whiff of Jace.

"We gotta go," Jace hoarsely whispered against his lips, his fingertips pressing into the curve of his ass.

Charlie moaned his disappointment into Jace's mouth and sucked his lips once more each, then pulled back to let Jace put him down. "We're saving that for later."

"Mmhmm," Jace grunted. He slipped a hand into his pocket, probably to adjust himself while he checked for his car keys, and Charlie had to do the same.

*Settle down there.*

Jesus, he hadn't even meant to kiss the guy before this party. Apparently they *weren't* just going as friends, although they still had no idea what they were.

"Take me all the way." When Jace's eyes widened and flicked to him, Charlie stuck out just the tip of his tongue and winked.

"You asshole," Jace laughed, turning to lead him out the front door to his car. "No distractions."

It was Charlie's turn to mock-nod. "Mmhmm."

"No groping me in public."

"Uh huh."

"You're not even listening, are you?" Jace complained.

Charlie tore his eyes off Jace's fine rear end. "What? Why would I want to? It *is* you talking."

Jace laughed richly and headed to the car while Charlie locked the front door.

Charlie's heart pounded with excitement as he tumbled into the passenger seat of the car and buckled up. He had to get his mind off Jace sometime, somehow, and an office party sounded like an awesome way of doing that.

An office party? *With* Jace? Where everyone would think they were together?

Yeah, Charlie could lie to himself a little longer and say he didn't want that.

---

It turned out office Christmas parties were boring as shit. This wasn't a party with the fire department, but the administrative department—and city hall employees were a lot more boring than Charlie had imagined.

Not that they were all in suits and ties. There were many in nice pullovers, like him. For once, he fit in perfectly with the rest of this crowd.

Jace introduced him as a friend to everyone who greeted him, and they all responded to him like Jace's new boyfriend anyway. Charlie didn't mind, because they gave him plenty of wine and cheese.

He stopped after the third glass, not wanting to look like a total wino. Especially given the ex-husband situation. Instead, he kept his hands busy by fidgeting with a plate of appetizers. Christmas cookies, fudge, spring rolls, and a tasty little macaroni and cheese tart with Parmesan topping...

"Hm? Sorry?" One of Jace's many colleagues was speaking to him. Jace had strode off to talk to some others while he was busy counting the mac-and-cheeses to make sure he had time to get another few.

"I said, your man has some balls of steel showing up today." There were four of them clustered around, all very office worker-esque. Hell, they could have come straight from the office, they were all dressed so boring.

"He's not my man, but I'll pass on the compliment to his balls," Charlie deadpanned, hoping to get a chuckle and move the conversation on from where he thought it was going.

No such luck.

"After the investigation..." another guy spoke up in an undertone.

"The one that found him not at fault?" Charlie knew staying quiet, walking away, would be better, but he couldn't help himself.

There was an uncomfortable shifting and nodding from the guys, but it was easy to tell they were bothered. Sure enough, seconds later, one of them spoke up again.

"Well, someone has to be at fault."

"Oh? Did you read it?" Charlie asked. He might never admit to Jace that he had read it, but he couldn't help himself. He had to know for himself. "It said there were regrettable circumstances, but nothing he should have been able to foresee. He has to take the fall for it because he's in charge, that's all, but the report cleared him."

"Mmm." One of the guys sipped his beer, glancing over toward him. "So you're the new boyfriend?"

*The new—I don't like that conversation shift, either.* "We're friends." Charlie smiled thinly, trying to remember who these guys were to him. A... manager of some department? He could have sworn another was some kind of council worker. Maybe not. Fuck, he should have paid more attention.

But he hadn't expected to be dragged into either of these conversations.

"Ahhh. You know about his divorce, then. Good for him. I figured after... well, you know. Anyone would want someone more respectable, like you." The guy tipped his beer slightly in a toast to him. "Sorry. Probably a sticky subject. My bad."

Charlie grudgingly nodded and didn't move in to clink his wine glass. "What do you mean?"

There was an uncomfortable, shifting silence between them all again.

One of the guys there took pity on him, putting a hand on

the most attitudinal guy's shoulder to do the talking himself. "You... You know he was with some druggie, right? It's been the talk of the department, I'm afraid. It all kind of came out during the investigation."

That sure as hell hadn't been in the report, but Charlie didn't let his expression shift.

"But a big shock even for us all. Mike's been there by his side forever. Finding out Mike was *that* kind of guy? Wow. Can't imagine what stress Jace was under that night, with that on his mind..." the fourth guy muttered while the other three nodded.

"Shame for him." Another guy shook his head. "He deserves better than some... lowlife druggie."

"I don't know much about Mike or how bad it was, but... so what?" Charlie frowned. "Lots of people are addicted to something or other. I don't know why that relationship broke down. Do you?"

Few things pissed him off more than people who would speak "politically correctly" about every other group they thought they were supposed to—often to cover up the thoughts they really still had about them—but saw addicts as some moral failures. It was in line with how they treated suicidal people, and mentally ill people, and... that was too personal. Too painful.

Fuck, no, he couldn't go on that rant.

"Oh, no, no. He doesn't talk about it. But he had to be upset if Mike fell off the wagon again..."

Charlie raised his brow. "He's not the type to let personal life interfere with work. Even I know that, and I haven't known him that long. If he had, I'm sure that would have been in the report. And I'm positive he wouldn't be thrilled to have it be the center of conversation tonight."

"Right, right. Yeah, my bad, man. No offense."

"You've given me good wine tonight," Charlie raised his glass with a slight smile. "So... none taken." He hoped he made his meaning clear: don't keep fucking pushing it.

When he glanced across the room, Jace was leaning on the doorframe overlooking the party, but Charlie could spot something nobody else did: the way he pressed his lips together, the tight double-handed grip on his wine glass.

Shit. Had he overheard some of this?

"'Scuse me," he told the group and strode off without waiting for an answer. He set his glass down at a table he passed, then joined Jace near the front door of the little event hall. "Fresh air?"

Jace's answer was strained. "Please."

Charlie steered him outside and around the side of the building to the small park. Four benches were arranged in a little square under a gazebo. When he cast a sharp glare at the woman who was smoking there, she put out her cigarette butt and headed back into the building, leaving them in peace.

"Shit," Jace breathed out as soon as the sound of clicking heels receded.

Charlie grabbed the glass from Jace's hand as it started to shake. "It's okay, baby," he breathed out, sinking onto the bench and pulling Jace down to sit next to him. "Just breathe through it. You're safe out here. Take your time."

"I didn't—I didn't mean to—fucking listen in... just..." Jace's sentences were short and choppy, his chest rising and falling in a rapid, staccato, irregular rhythm. He spread his knees and braced his elbows on them, then put his head in his hands. Tremors were coursing through his whole body now, his breathing harsh and audible. "C-Can't... breathe."

Charlie's heart twisted sharply, like glass shattering in his chest. He wanted to help—needed to help. Tears welled up for a second, but he blinked them away, focusing his attention on

Jace. He slid off the bench to kneel on the ground in front of Jace, covering his hands with his own. "Hey. Baby, listen to me."

Jace managed one slight nod. He was focusing on struggling to breathe, his breath coming in whining gasps. If he didn't know better, Charlie would say he was choking. The fact that it was on his own tension made Charlie's heart hurt.

Charlie gently laced his fingers with Jace's and pulled his hands down and away from his head gradually. He guided him until he rested flat along his knees, his hands in Charlie's. That way, if he passed out, he wouldn't smash his face on his own knees.

"C-Can't... focus..."

"Tell me what you're thinking. Give me a word or two. What's stuck in your head?" Charlie asked gently. He couldn't see Jace's face well, but crouched this close, he could hear every little catch in his breathing.

Jace hesitated for a few long seconds. Then, he breathed out in shallow gasps between silent pants, "Mike. Can't help him. Gonna get... get himself killed. Couldn't help Hans. Got him killed. Can't go back to work. Can't do it."

"Shh, shh," Charlie whispered, squeezing Jace's hands and rubbing them between his own. "Sweetie." *Oh, fuck. Stay calm yourself.* "Neither of them were your responsibility. You did the best you could with them both. Can you believe that? Or try?"

The concrete paving stones were hard on his knees and the air had a little bite to it without his jacket on, but he hardly noticed. He was flushed with heat from his concern for Jace.

Jace choked for a second but managed a tiny nod. For a mountain of a man, watching him crumpling into himself was more devastating than Charlie could ever put into words.

"Don't listen to those assholes," Charlie whispered. "The report had no reason to be biased in your favor. *That* didn't find you at fault at work. And it wasn't your responsibility to fix or save Mike, either, darling. Nobody can fix us except ourselves."

Jace pulled one hand back to cover his eyes, so Charlie let go of it to rub Jace's other hand gently between his palms and knead his fingers. He glanced away slightly, but there was no point in trying to give the man privacy when he was inches away, crowded up between his knees.

"Sorry. I didn't. I can't stop my brain... sometimes." Jace's voice wasn't wavering now, but his body still shuddered in quick, convulsive jolts. "The anxiety. It takes over my brain."

Charlie reached up to run his hand gently down Jace's back to the small of his back, then back up to his hair and scratched his scalp gently. "It's okay, darling. I told you. Take your time. Anxiety attacks are real."

"Didn't feel like. Doesn't. Feel like that. Felt like. Dying."

When a tandem guest panicked about the heights, Charlie had to be able to bring them to earth while they were still aloft. Being here on the ground made it a piece of cake.

But even from the hard-won syllables Jace tried to string together, Charlie felt his gut sink. It was no less real in someone's head than if they *were* facing their worst fear, the greatest danger to life and limb. That was the horrible part. He couldn't ever get between Jace and his own thoughts.

"I know," Charlie whispered. "But that's your brain playing tricks on you. You know that. Baby, you're safe. Nothing here's gonna get you. I'm staying with you until you're fine again."

Jace shuddered but nodded, pressing his lips tightly together to stop his jaw chattering. He pushed himself up on his elbow against his knees, and his face... it was stretched taut as if in pain.

"That's it. Breathe," Charlie whispered. "In for two, out for two. Make them a little deeper."

Jace followed his lead, hesitantly and slowly but surely.

He went from managing one or two breaths to a few in a row, and then Charlie talked him into breathing for three or four beats.

"I can't..." Jace shook his head, his teeth chattering for a moment. His body still shook at times, but it wasn't constant now. One hand still pressed against Charlie's, his fingers clutching tightly to Charlie's palm. "Can't do it. Go back to work there."

"Fuck 'em, then," Charlie whispered. "Well, not literally. I might get jealous."

The softest, barest chuckle from Jace, and Charlie's heart soared. *We're getting there. Oh, baby. I'm so fucking sorry, but you're getting there.*

"We'll figure out what to do if you can't go back to work there," Charlie followed up, still keeping his voice to a whisper. "But you know what? You might not feel strong, but you really are. You're almost over this attack, and you got there yourself. You might get to a point where you go back to feeling like the best damn fire chief they know."

Jace pulled his hands away slowly and sat up halfway, his eyes still closed as he braced his hands on his thighs. At last, he took a deep breath, then shook his head. "I'm... I think it's over. Fuck's sake, Charlie. I... that wasn't on my own. You..." he trailed off, hoarse with gratitude. "I. I... Yeah."

Charlie squeezed his knee, still kneeling between his legs and watching his expressions. "Don't mention it. Keep breathing. Your head doing better?"

"No runaway thoughts," Jace murmured. His expression was looser now, more natural, but his eyes were firmly closed. "I get those sometimes. And nightmares. And with that... and my baggage... my divorce..." he trailed off.

"Don't care," Charlie whispered. "Against the odds, I *like* you."

Jace's eyes flickered open, wide with shock, then doubt, as he scanned Charlie's face.

Though Charlie's own heart was flip-flopping with nervousness about what this meant, it felt so fucking right to say. Not just as a show to get him to calm down, but because it was the truth.

Then, Jace's expression softened again and he sat the rest of the way up. "Is that just because of your view right now?"

Charlie slumped with relief for a second, then grinned and tilted his chin up as he eyed the bulge from its best possible angle, then raked his gaze up to Jace's face again. "Well, the view doesn't hurt."

Jace's face still held too much gratitude and embarrassment to really follow through with their usual banter. Charlie pushed himself to his feet as Jace hauled him up onto the bench.

Jace's lips were warm on his, his kiss soft and almost chaste. No doubt his body was exhausted now, still half on-edge. Charlie kept his touch gentle.

"Fuck this party. Wanna go for a drive?" Jace murmured.

"Whatever you want, baby," Charlie whispered. "You okay to drive?" He couldn't look away from those gorgeous, dark eyes.

Jace offered him one of those sweet smiles. "With you there, I will be."

17

JACE

The hum of the steering wheel in his palms never failed to quiet Jace's nerves. Through it, he could feel the texture of the road itself under the car's wheels. It was hypnotic, and almost never sleep-inducing.

Maybe he ought to drive, calm himself down like a crying baby at night. That made him crack a grin to himself. That was a *little* harsh on him, but not untrue.

"I love it when the stars get all crisp in the winter. I mean, not that it's ever that cold out, but it's cool and fresh and... refreshing."

Jace appreciated Charlie making conversation with subjects he didn't have to talk much about. "Mm? You watch them a lot?"

"Yeah, now and then. I can't stay up late too much since I'm usually up early for work, but sometimes I'm up before the sun comes up and I see the last traces of night across the sky, and the ocean mirrors it on a calm night," Charlie sighed. "Gorgeous."

"I'd like to see that."

"I'll take you sometime," Charlie offered. He didn't seem too concerned with where they were going, so Jace drove on autopilot along one of his calming routes—up into the mountains of Santa Barbara.

The casino was up here, and not much else, but the views were stunning. Rolling green hills fading into the darkness, lights in the distance dotting the peaks, the warm glow of the town below disappearing into the winding road.

Few other cars were on the road, even at this relatively early evening hour, and the tranquillity of the moment between them blossomed.

"You like to just drive around like this?" Charlie asked after a few moments of gorgeous silence between them.

"Sometimes," Jace murmured. "Especially when I can't sleep."

"That's nice. I used to meditate. But now I have bad associations with that, too, so..." Charlie laughed sheepishly under his breath.

"Why?" Jace could keep up with listening, just couldn't form too many of his own words yet.

"Um. I was a mental case. Then I used meditation to, like, help when I got really depressed. Now I associate it with self-harm and... things."

"Ahhh." Jace slid one hand from the wheel to Charlie's knee and squeezed lightly. He understood perfectly that kind of association. God knew he had enough little mental links to Mike's life still. It might take him months or years to untangle them all, even after these months of separation.

That gave him an idea, but he wasn't sure if it was a good one. He cleared his throat. The radio was playing faint eighties rock, just low enough that it didn't interfere with their quiet conversation. Charlie stayed silent to let him speak.

"I, uh." His voice sounded strange even to himself, but he

was calm. The solidness of Charlie right there, listening to his every word, kept him grounded. "I have a blanket in the trunk."

"There are so many directions this can go, and only a few of them are disconcerting or wholly inappropriate in public..." Charlie trailed off, clicking his tongue. "Not that this is very public."

Jace managed a laugh, squeezing Charlie's knee. "We could head down to the beach, and—"

"Sold." Charlie rested his hand over Jace's and smiled. "Take me wherever you want to go."

Jace turned around at a pull-off and headed back down, threading through the mountain pass toward the lights of the city before turning away to follow the highway along the coast. He could already hear the surf and smell the ocean breeze through the half-open car windows.

He picked a beach and parked, relieved to see no other cars there. Teens necking in the woods wouldn't improve this experience.

"Nice," Charlie smiled. "I wish I could fly here. Conditions aren't right. I don't get to enough beaches that *aren't* flying spots for me, really." He bent over to take off his shoes.

Jace drew a breath and unbuckled, then did the same. As he worked through the laces, he formed the perfect sentence. At last, shoes set aside, he shut off the car and turned to Charlie. "Are you sure you want to be doing this with me?"

Charlie, silenced from his rambling train of thought, stared through the dark car at him, his brow furrowed lightly as if trying to work out what Jace meant. "Huh? Why not? This, as in...?"

"Dealing with my crazy," Jace said flatly. Now that he was calm again, humiliation crept into his chest and twisted his gut, making him not quite able to meet Charlie's eyes. "It was good of you back there to. But—"

"I'm not all fun and merriment, either," Charlie cut him off, unbuckling and shifting to sit sideways, pulling up a knee beside himself. "Darling..." Then, he went red. Even in the semi-darkness, it was easy to see from the way he dipped his head, flustered for a second. "Uh. I hope you don't mind that."

Something deep in Jace's chest glowed. The affectionate names were one of those things he'd missed the most. "I don't mind," he murmured, twisting sideways himself. He'd heard Charlie call other people—all four of the grooms, and their friends—pet names if he knew them well enough. Before tonight, and before they'd fucked, he hadn't given one to Jace.

"Jace," Charlie resumed, his voice stronger, "I'm a mess, too. I hide it well, but I'm not all there. And I..." he breathed out heavily, then laughed quietly.

"What?"

"I can't believe I'm telling you this. All my problems and shit."

Jace cracked a quiet smile. "Ditto me and mine."

Charlie nodded slightly, then reached out to run a hand down Jace's arm. Jace turned his hand face-up to let Charlie's fingers caress his palm. "But you have damn good reason to have problems. I mean, I can't imagine whatever happened with the divorce, plus your work stress, both at the same time. You're exceptionally strong to have made it through that."

"I don't feel it," Jace whispered, the truth coming a little too easily under the spell of ocean waves and darkness. He even managed to meet Charlie's eyes while he said it, his heart starting to hammer.

Charlie shifted out of his seat, and Jace realized he was coming over toward him, awkwardly clambering over the console between them. This at least gave the perfect distraction after his confession. He laughed as Charlie's ass hit the steering wheel and made the horn honk for a split second.

"Jesus!" Charlie exclaimed, thrusting his hips toward Jace and away from the wheel, then flipping it off over his shoulder.

Jace just laughed louder. He pushed his seat all the way back, then closed his legs so Charlie had room on his seat to straddle him.

It wasn't perfect, but it worked—Charlie crouched over his lap, fingers combing through his hair, his weight resting on Jace's knees.

Oh, God. The weight felt *good*.

Charlie pressed a kiss against Jace's lips, the warm taste of him making Jace's eyelids flutter shut instinctively. The pressure of damp skin against his own, the tongue flickering, every sensation easily felt... it gave him a single point of contact to focus on among the incredible buzzy feeling of having this man blanket him.

He slid his arms around Charlie's waist and hummed under his breath, rubbing up and down his back slowly.

*Maybe I didn't realize how fucking starved for touch I was. Maybe I have been for a long time.*

Mike would be by his side at events, sure. And he'd give him shoulder-rubs at home, and they fucked a lot—before this last year, when things got weird and rough between them—but Mike hadn't been a cuddler.

Jace suddenly needed Charlie not to pull back. He looped his arms hard around Charlie's back until their crotches pressed, their chests close together.

Charlie made a small sound of surprise but smiled against his lips, then pressed a few gentler kisses against his jaw and neck before burying his face in Jace's shoulder. "I don't feel strong, either," Charlie murmured. "There's... ex shit, you know a bit about that. And family shit. All kinds of shit I haven't told you about."

Jace loosened his hold just enough to rub Charlie's back

again. "And I haven't properly told you about Mike or the fire or any of it."

"You need to talk," Charlie murmured.

"So do you."

"Not more than you," Charlie whispered. He turned his head, his nose pressing into Jace's neck until his hot breath on Jace's skin made Jace shiver and chuckle. "So talk. I've got all night."

Jace thought about it for a second, but his body was already relaxing. He could fucking stay like this all night. Charlie's back might get a little sore after a while, but the thought of pulling away...

His chest was tight. "It's my fault. I know... I *know* it isn't... but it feels like it is. I can't ever... I don't mean to harp on it, to drag myself through self-pity, but he was *mine*, and I let him walk into danger."

"Who?" Charlie whispered.

Jace flinched, then chuckled quietly. "Good point. Both of them."

Charlie swallowed hard but stayed still and silent.

Jace went on. "And I had to face his family, and a courtroom, and... well. Mike got away, he can *do* something, be something, if he chooses... but Hans..."

Hans had been barely out of training academy, rotating between fire houses to learn all the duties and districts. Jace had been about to assign him to work with Liam, Chris, and Kevin, because he trusted them to keep him safe.

But he'd been the one to let him down.

"That night, he should have had another supply line. We didn't know there was a mechanical failure with his. I should have sent someone with more experience in, but Chris was trapped and Liam couldn't have done it, and he was the only one who was there and ready. He couldn't read the conditions."

Jace's lips were numb as he rolled his head back against the seat. "The wind picked up. When we got the back door open, it's... think of an oven. That effect. Our suits are good, but they're not perfect." It was simplifying the situation, but in civilian terms, it was the best way he could explain it without losing his shit. "There were more things, but those were the big ones. He didn't make it to the guy he was trying to rescue. He should have made it out. It wasn't supposed to be..." Jace trailed off.

His throat was tight, and he didn't think he could manage any more words.

"Baby. Hon, look at me," Charlie whispered, his hand running up Jace's chest to his shoulder. He squeezed at the muscle between his shoulder and neck, rubbing the tension out of his traps before caressing his jaw with his thumbs until Jace relented and opened his eyes. When Jace was confident he wasn't going to tear up and he did so, Charlie was there, gazing at him with such understanding.

"Sorry," Jace managed with a tight little chuckle. "Gotta be hard to hear."

Charlie shook his head. "Have you talked to anyone else about it?"

"Not Mike... I'd already kicked him out," Jace whispered, his eyes half-closing again at the memory of that night. The first long night—after paperwork and formal identification of the body and family calls, after media and all layers of management, after checking on those of his men in the hospital...

Alone in the utterly silent house, wishing for even a drugged-up, incomprehensible Mike. A warm body to hold and be held by.

Someone to tell him it wasn't his fault.

"It's not your fault," Charlie whispered, and he was back in the present, blinking tears out of his eyes again. "Oh, baby. I know it's hard to believe, but you said it yourself. Hard conditions. Other people were at fault. You can't make everyone's judgement calls all day long. He chose to work this job."

"It's not his fault he's dead."

Charlie stubbornly murmured, "Then it's not yours, either." He wouldn't back down when Jace glared at him.

*How does he know? He wasn't there.* Jace worked through the first resentful thoughts, gritting his teeth as he worked his jaw around and fought the instinct to argue about it.

Charlie was rubbing the back of his neck slowly, scratching the hair at the back of his head, and it was too fucking impossible to be angry. Not with the little emotional reserve he had left.

"Fine," Jace whispered. He cleared his throat and shook his head. "I'm in therapy. For work. Took time off. All that stuff."

"Good," Charlie murmured. "Don't let yourself get to that dark place alone. You're not the only chief to have lost one of his team, I'm sure of it."

Jace drew a long breath and let it out, then turned his head so his nose pressed into Charlie's hair. "Your cologne smells nice." It was light, airy, so delicate he'd almost questioned whether it were just his natural scent.

Charlie paused for a second, then laughed under his breath. "Thanks."

"No, thank you," Jace murmured. He cleared his throat, raising his hand to cup the back of his neck again. "And, uh. Me too."

Charlie went silent for a second, trying to work out what he meant. It wasn't even part of this conversation, so Jace couldn't blame him.

But holy shit, Jace's palms were sweaty at even saying *this* much. He couldn't bring himself to finish the sentence and mirror Charlie's confession...

*Against the odds, I like you.*

"Against the odds," Jace breathed out.

He felt Charlie's quick inhale, the tension that hit him for a second, and then a tremor of... what? Excitement? Nervous anticipation? "Oh," Charlie breathed out. "Ah."

Shit. Oh, fuck, what if he'd been being nice just to help him get through that moment? "Unless you were just—"

"Shut the fuck up," Charlie told him in a quite calm and pleasant tone that made Jace bark a quick laugh. "No take-backsies. And don't make me say it again."

"I..." Jace trailed off, then laughed again. "Okay." He hugged Charlie until Charlie couldn't breathe and slapped his shoulder.

"Oooof. Dude. Don't break my fucking rib, either. Get that blanket and let's get down to the beach before my ass honks again."

"Ew. At least the windows are down," Jace grinned, pushing open the car door and staying still while Charlie squirmed off his lap.

His heart still pounded at the idea of Charlie *knowing* all of this about him—knowing his weak spots, his darkest moments.

But it also felt completely, perfectly right to let him in. Where Charlie wore his heart on his sleeve, Jace had never trusted his heart enough. Maybe he could stand to be a little more like Charlie.

Who already had the blanket from the trunk and was waving it at him, trotting down to the beach as Jace snapped out of his thoughts.

"Hey. Wait up," Jace protested, laughing and pocketing his keys as he slammed the car door shut.

The beach sand was soft and cool underfoot, but pleasant. Bits of gravel, pieces of dried seaweed—none of it bothered Jace too much. The sand was smooth and clean past the tideline.

When he reached the blanket, he smiled at the sight of Charlie already sitting cross-legged on it, then crashed next to him.

As he sank down, Charlie scooted close until they were leaning on each other like fire logs in a teepee, the flame between them sparking to life.

He had no idea where this was going, but he liked it. This was the right move. It was nothing like bringing Mike down here to sober up. It was...

It was something new, and different, and wonderful.

## CHARLIE

It was Charlie's second shower in twelve hours.

Last night, after they cuddled on the beach for an hour, Jace had dropped him off and he'd showered for two reasons: first, to get the sand out of his toes and hair, and second, for a poor substitute to Jace's warmth in the chilly evening, Jace's arms wrapped around him, the side of Jace's head pressing into Charlie's shoulder.

Now, he needed to wake up and stop daydreaming about Jace. He had to visit his dad today and find out how he liked the extra support. Knowing his dad, he didn't.

Charlie hummed all the way to Pine Grove, the sobriety of the moment only settling in once he reached the parking lot.

It took a toll on him to be cheerful and keep a good face on for his dad, day in and day out.

Sometimes his dad had a good day, and he seemed to know newer things—he talked about his friends at the home, or asked how Charlie's work was coming along, and he didn't mention Justin.

Other days, it seemed like the rest of him had carried on

but his mind had had enough and chosen one second several years ago to exist in, forever.

"Good morning," he greeted Jenny, who was behind the desk, chatting with Karen.

"Oh, Charles. Good to see you." Jenny came around the desk with a warm smile for him. "Here to see your dad?"

"Yep."

"Okay. Just to let you know, he's a bit... out of sorts today," Jenny gently cautioned, walking with him down the hall toward his dad's room.

Charlie sighed. "Yeah. Okay. Thanks."

Jenny patted his back. "But it's good of you to come. I don't think he knows how close to the holidays it is, but he's been enjoying the carols. We have a piano player coming in every evening for them."

That sounded peaceful, if Charlie didn't think too much about it. He'd visited the living room area with his dad before, and it was hard to be there. Some residents didn't seem to engage with anyone, while others were loud or impulsive, speaking suddenly or grabbing your arm as you passed. Some had food restrictions, so bringing in food was hard.

*God bless the nurses of the world.* Charlie gave her an appreciative smile. "Thank you. For everything."

"Of course." They were at his dad's room, and Jenny gently knocked. "Gregory? Your son's here to see you." She pushed the door open.

"Which one?"

"Charles."

"Oh, Charles—Charlie boy, Charles..." His dad was in a wheelchair near the window. "Come in."

Charlie hadn't seen his dad in one since he'd had minor surgery about four years ago. He'd gotten out of it as soon as possible and swore never to go back in one.

"Look at this thing they have me in!" His dad flapped a hand at Jenny. "We're fine, I want to see him," he dismissed.

He *was* on edge, then. Charles cast her an apologetic look but she just smiled and closed the door after herself.

"What do you have them putting me in this for?"

Charles sighed as he headed to the window, grabbing a chair for himself. "I'm sorry, Dad. I know it's annoying."

"Everyone wheels me around. Don't even ask," his dad grumbled, mostly to himself, his gaze fixed out the window.

That *did* sound annoying to Charles. But he'd also watched the nursing staff with other patients. They always told them or asked before they moved someone's chair. Was his dad struggling to hear, too?

He lowered his voice. "Has anything fun been going on?"

Dad didn't react—just stared out the window.

Charles couldn't tell if he was angry at him, if the resentment over the mobility assistance was being aimed at him, or if he was just not hearing. He tried again.

"Anything fun going on here?"

"I heard you. Why didn't you bring Justin?"

"He's..." Charlie trailed off, then touched his face and rubbed his chin. "Not around, Dad."

"Shame. He wouldn't have put me in this thing."

Charles caught his breath, heat rushing through his cheeks as he curled his fingers around the arms of his chair. "No. He'd just let you fall."

"What?" His dad fixed him with a glare now, and Charles flinched. His dad went on. "You know, I'm fine on my own. Even if Jemma and Brian never come. Just fine."

"I'll call them, if—"

"It's not about them, damn it, boy!"

His dad got into these moods sometimes. It was frustration —the fists and teeth of his anger clashing against the bars that held him in place. Charles knew that, but it made it no easier to watch or bear the brunt of.

"I know." Charles swallowed hard past the lump in his throat.

"I liked Justin. He talked to me more than you did before I came here."

Charles couldn't hold back his flinch. For the thousandth time, he wondered if it was worth it.

But... no. It wouldn't help anyone. His dad was already angry. Best-case scenario, he understood why Charlie had left Justin, and he'd just be angrier about it. Worst-case scenario, he had to have the same conversation over and over.

"I'd better go. I have work today, Dad. I love you."

His dad sullenly stared back out the window, his fingers tight on the arms of his chair. Charlie glanced back over his shoulder but he hadn't moved by the time he got to the door.

He drew a quick sigh and let it out once he was in the hallway, the door closed against his dad's temper, but not his own thoughts and memories.

Justin *had* talked to his dad a lot. They'd bonded over fixing cars, drinking beer and watching football, all those manly things. Charlie had been glad, at first, because his dad wholeheartedly took Justin in like any son-in-law, and he'd feared worse.

But then it had become a trap. Justin had been close enough to his dad that he couldn't talk to him about what was happening. The bruises were explained away every time before he even got to see his dad, the arguments presented carefully so his own dad wouldn't take his side—would just stay neutral.

And slowly, his world had narrowed until Justin was the center of it and the only thing he had. Justin controlled his work hours—so he didn't work too much and stress himself out —and his money and...

Charlie almost didn't notice the nurses wishing him a good day. He distractedly raised a hand in a wave, walking to the car on autopilot.

Leaving Justin hadn't stopped the demons in his own head. Every whisper in the night about how he was lucky that Justin loved him, because he was so pretty... every "apology" for how sensitive Charlie was and how he'd misinterpreted his words... every action carefully designed to make him feel unlovable, unworthy, with Justin as his only solution.

Justin had been there for him, taking the razor blade out of his hands, but he'd replaced it with his own punishments.

Charlie swallowed back the memory for just long enough to call Jemma. He only had a few minutes before work.

"Hey, little brother. What's up?"

"Are you busy?"

"Yeah, just on my way out the door. Why?"

Charlie let out a quick sigh. "Sorry. We should talk about Dad. He's in a wheelchair now, at the home. He's falling more. You should go see him."

"I will." Voices in the background—Jemma's kids. They kept her busy half the day, and her law work the other half. God knew when she slept. Charlie felt bad bothering her. "As soon as I can."

"Okay. Thanks. I'm gonna call Brian, too."

Jemma snorted. "Good luck with that. Let me know if you need backup."

"Thanks, sis." Charlie hung up and breathed a quiet sigh. She was right.

Brian was the one without commitments, but still, he managed to find ways not to be here for holidays, not to see his dad for his birthday... nothing. He'd shut out the idea long ago, and he obviously couldn't stand seeing him like this.

But Jemma's new, busy life and Brian's carefree attitude

meant Charlie was the one stuck here with his dad, doing it all and paying for it all.

Sure enough, he only got Brian's voicemail. He left a quick message for him to call him back, but he didn't expect to hear back. Brian was good at sensing when there was a problem—especially financial—and dropping off the radar.

God knew he'd done that when Charlie broke up with Justin. Jemma had seen it, had tried to help, but she'd been just giving birth to the twins, and Charlie couldn't add more stress to her life, so he'd underplayed it to her.

That was Justin back on his mind, crawling in there like a snake, through every fucking thought he could. Justin's voice reminding him at strategic moments how much his dad liked him, how glad he was that his dad had taken him in since his own parents lived far away, and it hurt to be far away from his parents... how could anyone take away what bit of family he'd found?

"Fuck it," Charlie muttered. The glider was already on hand for the lessons later. He could get a quick flight of his own in, and a good adrenaline thrill was just what he needed to get his brain clear.

He opted for a foot-powered launch, which meant cliff-jumping.

There was no better escape from his thoughts than running down a grassy meadow, the lightweight frame stiff against him, the wind resistance already strong, knowing the ground was going to drop away from his feet any second.

He perfectly understood what Ash had felt. The difference was that he'd had one too many commitments—his dad, that was it—to do it without strapping a glider to himself first and giving himself a fair chance at survival.

Despite the temptation, he circled to the updraft to get above it—to rise, and rise, and rise.

Charles had to be high to get the best jolt out of falling, and the aching pleasure that settled into his bones. If it was a subtler, less scarring self-harm he'd found now, he'd take it.

On he rose.

---

The tandem flights were one after the other, neither of them a challenge. Breaking it down took very little time, even on his own. He hadn't asked Hannah to come in, with just these couple of easy flights to do.

Just as well. Once he dropped his peppy gliding expert façade, he wasn't good company even to himself. The flight earlier had taken the worst of the sting out of his need to hurt himself, but it was still there.

It seemed crazy to call after not even a day apart, but Charles couldn't help himself.

"Hey, Jace here."

The warm voice that thrummed through the phone line instantly soothed him as he leaned back in the driver's seat of his car. "Hey. I just finished up my flights."

"You want me to come over for lunch?"

Jace had no idea how well-timed his question was... or maybe he did. "Yeah," Charlie agreed instantly. "I'll be right home."

True to his word, he broke a speed limit or two to get home before Jace arrived, and he even managed to get chicken breasts and rice in the oven before the doorbell rang.

Jace—in another hot, clingy t-shirt, of course—had a binder under his arm. "Hey." He noticed Charlie's look right away. "I wasn't sure if you wanted silent company or talk-ative company, so I brought this in case you told me to shut up."

Charlie cracked his first real grin all day, then laughed lightly. "I'll accept your noise-making if I need to."

"Mmm. I bet you will."

"Talking, I mean." Charlie snorted and went to grab placemats.

"You know I can do that," Jace teased.

His mouth *was* pretty dirty in bed, true, but Charlie hadn't meant to hit on him that fast. "Oh, cool it and grab the utensils."

"Aye aye, sir," Jace teased, but as he passed Charlie, he pulled him in to hug him around the waist and kiss him. "You had fun last night?" He let go to let him put down the placemats.

Charlie didn't want to pull away. "Yeah. You?"

"Yeah."

Jace looked a lot better today—less anxious and stressed, that was for sure.

That made Charlie feel more confident in his next question. "Is that for work?" Charlie asked. "Or is it wedding planning? It looks pretty damn thick—don't—"

"I didn't!"

"—to be wedding planning."

"The thicker it is, the quicker the wedding."

Charlie cracked up, his jaw dropping as he turned to Jace. "You *are* filthy! I knew it."

Jace gave him a roguish wink. "It's you rubbing off on me. As often as possible." He ran a hand up his stomach to give Charlie a peek at those washboard abs that felt *so* good to grind against...

No, he was distracting him. Charlie flipped him off and headed back to the kitchen to check on their lunch. "I know what you're doing."

"Damn." Jace stretched his legs out and opened the binder.

"In answer to your question, yes, it's work. Reviewing some recent incident reports to see what I missed while I was away."

"Oof. Sounds heavy."

"A little," Jace agreed.

Still, the company was easy as Charlie finished cooking and Jace finished his work. And when they'd finished lunch and brought the dishes to the kitchen, neither of them made a move to continue with their chores.

Instead, Charlie nodded to the couch and Jace took his hand to lead him there.

"So, what was up this morning?" Jace asked when they were settled, arms around each other.

Charlie closed his eyes and sighed, the exhaustion and frustration creeping into the edges of his good mood. It nibbled away at the joy that felt rounded and airy within him.

"There's a lot to explain."

"Hit me with it," Jace murmured. "I've got all day."

Charlie ran his hand slowly down Jace's thigh to his knee, then picked up his hand and rubbed it between his own before starting to play with his fingers. The tactile contact and having something to do with his hands helped.

"I went to see my dad. He lives in an assisted living home just outside the city." Jace sucked in a small, sympathetic breath but stayed quiet, which he appreciated. "His memory... he's got dementia. He's sort of stuck in the past sometimes. Gets moody, angry about things. Takes it out on me."

"I'm sorry," Jace whispered, pressing his lips into Charlie's hair.

"Asks about my ex, who he liked better than me."

Jace swallowed hard. "Is this the one that...?" he trailed off, his body hard and tense suddenly. His arm was tight and protective.

Charlie rubbed Jace's thumb slowly until he relaxed, then

touched his nails. Clean, short—a working man's hands even if he was off right now. His chest was tight, and he didn't focus on his own thoughts again. He'd done that enough earlier. "Yeah."

"Shit. I'm sorry."

Charlie could feel the fury in Jace's body as he spoke those words. He knew how to identify it right away—knew how to tell if someone pressing into him was lustful, furious, or both. That was thanks to Justin, too.

"If you want to talk about it," Jace added, his voice careful and measured, "I'll listen. And I won't even threaten him too much."

Charlie breathed out a quick laugh of appreciation. The idea of Jace hurting someone on his behalf... made his stomach turn. Seeing that same potential in Jace, even against someone who had hurt *him*, would be hard to watch. Even hearing it in his voice was difficult.

"There's not a lot to say. We dated for too long. He isolated me, shut me off from everyone. My siblings—little brother, older sister—didn't even realize what was happening. He won my dad over. He made me think it was because he loved me too much, too fiercely to control..." Charlie trailed off.

Fuck. His fingers were laced with Jace's and he was holding his hand so hard it had to hurt him. When he tried to relax his grip, Jace just squeezed back.

Charlie's eyes stung. "So when he didn't hurt me, I hurt myself. Stopped that—physically, I mean—a couple years back, a little while after I left him. Never got help for it, really, but once I was out of that place... well, no. I'm tempted still, sometimes. I do, um. I push myself."

God, he was spilling it all, but Jace was just holding him, his breath warm on his cheek, rubbing his shoulder very slightly with his other thumb. The tiny move spoke of volumes of affection Charlie wasn't sure he could handle.

"It's a cloud. It's lifting, slowly. I have bad days. Very bad days. I don't... I can't always control them," Charlie murmured. His nose was wet, and so was his chin. He swiped at his eyes, annoyed for the distraction. "But I know already that what he did, said, was wrong. It's just..."

"It takes time," Jace spoke up at last, his voice hoarse. "Babe. Fuck. I'm sorry." Charlie had used the pet name once for him, but it was the first time he could remember Jace using it.

He glowed with pleasure, despite the rush of other emotions flooding his body—the old pain and grief, the new layers of insight that had peeled them open.

*He doesn't just want me. He's here for me in return. It's... reciprocal.*

"I... Thank you," Charlie murmured, trying to wrap his mind around what he'd just thought.

Jace pressed his lips into Charlie's hair and squeezed him hard, almost crushing him against his chest. "Of course. I don't wanna see you... hurt, or hurting, again. I guessed something was up, but... fuck."

"Yeah. Butt fuck," Charlie agreed breathlessly. His eyes were stinging but dry now. "That helps."

Jace laughed quietly, but he just kept Charlie against him. "I'd rather kiss you. Can I?"

*I really like him. Oh, fuck.* Charlie couldn't remember the last time someone had asked to kiss him, and he'd felt the *yes* flood through his whole body before it ever made it to his lips.

"Yes," he breathed out, shifting against Jace until their knees knocked and their hips pushed into each other. Straddling Jace's lap was one of his favorite places to be.

Their lips and hands explored, but it wasn't rough, and it wasn't with a purpose. It wasn't even exploration, really. They'd kissed slow and sweetly before.

It was something else altogether, some weird uneven footing between them that held them back from just fucking on the nearest surface and walling off the thoughts they'd shared over the last day.

Whatever it was, it was precious, fragile, and terrifying.

JACE

It was a good thing Charlie had a job, because Jace would have spent day after day in his house, losing all track of time.

As it was, he had to go home to get fresh clothes after his unexpected night at Charlie's place, and Charlie had a few customers to work with. It gave him a chance to clean the house, which he did to keep his nerves steady.

He wanted to rip that Justin bastard to shreds, wanted to turn him in to the cops and make him feel even an ounce of the pain he deserved. But he held back those words and impulses, and let Charlie find safety in him instead of a vengeful protector.

The call couldn't come soon enough. Just like yesterday, he nearly lunged for his phone when it rang with Charlie's ringtone.

Unlike yesterday, Charlie sounded more upbeat when he greeted him. "Hey, it's me."

"Coming over?"

"Ooh, do I get to see your place now?"

Jace groaned. "If you don't trash it."

"I'll keep my paper-shredding in check, cross my heart. Be there in half an hour. Don't spend the whole time cleaning."

"I wouldn't dream of it. My place is always clean," Jace retorted.

Charlie snorted. "Fine. You win, for now. See you, babe." The pet name rolled so easily from his tongue, like he'd been saying it for months.

Jace's heart always skipped a beat. Mike hadn't been so free with those names, except when he was trying to earn a smile from Jace after doing something stupid.

He wandered around the living room, tidying everything up and then moving things around slightly so it didn't look *worryingly* clean. Between that distraction and his own thoughts about Charlie, he lost track of time until the knock on the door.

"Hey!" He tried not to sound overeager as he pulled open the door to let Charlie in, examining him to see how he looked.

"Hey yourself." Charlie's face was relaxed, his shoulders down and eyes bright. *Much better,* Jace concluded and beamed at him.

"Beer? Soda? Water?"

"You're trying to drown me and I'm not even fully inside your house yet."

Jace winked, but stepped aside to close the door after him. "Gotta hydrate you before I can dehydrate you. We did leave things hanging the other night, considering our pre-Christmas party plans..."

Charlie squinted at him and kicked off his shoes, then looped their arms together loosely. "The first time over at your house, and you hit on me before you even show me where the kitchen is. Who are you and what have you done with Jace?"

"Why, are you offering to make sandwiches afterward?" Jace was fully expecting the punch to the stomach that he got, but he didn't expect it to be so light. "I'm kidding," he grinned. "Mostly."

Charlie scoffed. "Good thing you're hot."

Jace's cheeks flushed, and he tried not to take it as too much of a compliment. It was just part of their banter. "So, the bedroom with ensuite is upstairs, if you're wondering. Kitchen's this way. Here's the living room. The bathroom's through there, for future reference, when we have wild animal sex on the couch..."

Despite himself, Charlie melted against Jace with laughter, his body weight pressing into Jace's shoulder as he freely trusted him to hold him up. "You really are coming unbuttoned."

"I think that's one hundred percent your fault." Jace spun Charlie around and pulled him in sharply against his front, looping his arms around his waist.

Despite himself, he was giddy. He was fucking giddy as fuck to see Charlie, and they'd only said goodbye—with a goodbye kiss—that morning. Oh, man. He was so screwed.

"I'll accept *full* blame," Charlie breathed out, leaning in to press their lips together. They kissed slowly despite their quick banter, lips and tongues softly finding each other, hands pressing at the smalls of each other's backs, but not groping.

When they pulled apart, Jace kept his eyes closed for a second too long. He already ached for another taste of those sweet, full lips.

"I could use a glass of water, if that's what we're going for."

Jace smiled at Charlie. "Do you want to?"

"What kind of stupid question's that?" Charlie grumbled, which made Jace laugh. "Turn down sex? Me?"

"Now you're calling yourself easy again." Jace clicked his tongue. "You can't blame me for that one."

"Maybe I am." Something flickered in Charlie's eyes, and he watched Jace closely.

*I don't know what he's looking for from me.* Jace just looked back, closely studying Charlie for a few moments. "Okay. So?"

That had been the right answer, apparently. Charlie breathed a quick laugh and half-smiled at him. Then, he pulled away to stride for the kitchen. "Water?"

"Yeah. Please."

Jace leaned against the doorway, watching Charlie open a couple cupboards until he found the glasses.

It felt easy and comfortable between them. Every step of... whatever this was... seemed to.

Was this how friends-with-benefits worked these days? When Charlie had said he liked him... how far did that go? God, he was out of the dating loop.

He accepted the glass of water and drank up, watching Charlie look around his kitchen.

"This is a really nice place," Charlie finally concluded with a bright smile. "It suits you."

"I think I'll take that as a compliment," Jace winked. It was homey, that was for sure. Especially since Mike left, he'd taken extra care to replace everything Mike had taken with him with something that *he* liked. His own style, his own place, his own life.

The one thing he had going now.

"You'd better. I'm not just handing them out because I like you," Charlie waved a hand, setting down his empty water glass and striding for the stairs. "Bedroom's this way?"

A slow grin spread over Jace's face, his eyes on the way those jeans clung to Charlie's ass. God, it looked good. "I like that take-charge attitude." He barely lasted three steps on the stairs until he was reaching out to grab a handful of the goods, then slid his hand around to grope him.

Charlie moaned and paused on the step for half a second, pushing back into Jace as he gripped the handrail with the other hand. Their bodies crushed together for a few moments as Jace ground against Charlie, then leaned in over his shoulder for a kiss.

Charlie kissed him *hard*, all the teeth and spitfire that had been missing from their hello kiss suddenly back.

*I like this side of him, too. I fucking like every side of him.* Jace growled lowly and pushed against Charlie, half-tempted to sling him over his shoulder right now.

Charlie's eyes glinted like he knew what Jace wanted. He stood his ground, slowly turning against Jace until their chests pressed together.

They couldn't keep away from each other's lips now, their wet lips sliding easily together.

"Do I have to say the password to get up the stairs?" Jace whispered hoarsely against Charlie's mouth. He sucked Charlie's lower lip between his before he could answer, slowly running his tongue along it until he felt the tremble in Charlie's thighs.

When he let go, Charlie managed a quiet grunt. "N-Nope."

His mind flickering over what to say next, Jace had another idea. Instead of saying anything at all, he sank to his knees on the stairs.

It was fucking impulsive, but what had he done with Charlie so far that *wasn't*? He was also getting hard on the spot, and the way Charlie's jaw dropped made it worth it.

"I wasn't expecting..." Charlie trailed off, his voice faint.

Jace grinned, already sliding Charlie's zipper down. "I know you weren't." It took him seconds before he had Charlie's jeans and underwear down around his thighs, that gorgeous cock hardening in his very hand.

Seconds more before his lips were wrapped around the tip,

sucking Charlie's manhood into his mouth and teasing it with his tongue as it swelled under the attention. This was the hottest stage of a blowjob—this or the end, the desperate half-thrusts when Charlie made all the desperate, needy sounds he recalled so well in his morning showers.

He bobbed his head quickly, spreading wetness down the shaft and keeping his lips firmly clamped around the skin. Wringing pleasure out of Charlie was as easy as pie. Charlie was already slumping, trying to hold himself up against the wall.

Jace was extra-careful as Charlie's knees buckled, grabbing his hips to push him down onto the stairs. He climbed one more step up, bracing his knees on the stairs before sucking Charlie's cock back into his mouth like it was the only thing he wanted.

And it was. Right now, all he wanted was to make Charlie *writhe* in pleasure against the stairs, right out in the open, his hips shuddering as he gasped for breath...

"St-Stop. Jesus," Charlie moaned, still gripping the handrail tightly with one hand, the other on the edge of the stair.

Jace pulled back sharply, his breath catching. Had his teeth scraped? He couldn't be that bad—

"I'm going to be pissed as *hell* if I come without your dick in me."

Jace's eyes widened, and then he grinned. "What's the rush? We have all day."

"*Jace.*"

The way Charlie spun his name, sharpened the *J* and gritted out the *ace* put a whole sentence of meaning into a single syllable.

Jace couldn't remember *anyone* having said his name like that before.

Without another word, he grabbed Charlie and slung him

over his shoulder with the effortless grace of his training. He still had that, too—his workouts.

"Oh my God, you nearly made me come again just there," Charlie moaned. His hard cock dug into Jace's shoulder, bare ass up in the air. What a sight.

Jace rubbed over the rounded, firm mounds. He slapped lightly but firmly, a touch of scolding. "No coming. Not until my cock's in you. You said it yourself."

"Oh, *yes*, siiir." Charlie's tone was designed to get under his skin. "You're the boss."

Jace dumped him on the bed and collapsed over him, already kissing that smart mouth of his again. If Charlie didn't piss him off so much, he'd say he loved it. "Do you want me to be?" he breathed out, nipping Charlie's ear.

When he glanced at Charlie again, his eyes had lit up, dark and wide and fixed on him. "Yes."

Jace flipped Charlie onto his front, kissing his way from behind his ear down to the back of his neck. He peeled Charlie's t-shirt off in a quick jerk, then his own, and hauled their pants off just as fast.

He needed them both naked.

"*This*," Charlie panted, "is fucking hot. I knew you had this in you."

Jace grabbed Charlie's wrists, pinning them against his back in one hand. "Yeah?"

"Fuck. Yes!" Charlie squirmed against him, spreading his knees, his breathing already fast. "Jace, please. Fuck, you're going to tease me, aren't you? Don't fucking tease me...! Please. Fuck..."

Jace pressed a few more slow kisses along the back of his neck, around to his chin, while Charlie begged. "You've got me riled up so easily now. It's fucking insane. I wanna do the same to you. I want you on the edge for *hours*, one of these days."

The whimper that escaped Charlie was almost inhuman. Charlie pushed up into him again, grinding against his dick and reminding him exactly what he wanted—needed—so badly it was starting to hurt.

Fine. Charlie would get his way tonight, but Jace was done pretending he wasn't planning for a *next time*. There had already been several next times for them, and he didn't see them stopping any time soon.

And it thrilled him.

Jace kissed slowly down Charlie's spine, savoring the faintly salty taste as he sweated, writhed against the bed, and clearly desperately tried not to grind against it.

When he'd reached Charlie's wrists, Jace kissed the back of his hand and then skipped over them, keeping his grip tight. He pressed a kiss to one firm ass cheek, then the other. "You have a gorgeous ass."

"Th-Thanks," Charlie breathed out, his voice wavering. "But more importantly, I'm gonna come all over your goddamn bed."

"No, you won't."

"*Hrrrrgh.*" The growl of frustration was too fucking cute, and Jace grinned at it. "I fucking *hate* you right now."

"I bet you do," Jace purred. "You'll hate me a little less in a second." He ran his tongue down the valley between those gorgeous cheeks, circling that tight hole but not yet touching it, just to tease him for a moment more.

"*Jace!* FuckfuckfuckJace...!"

Charlie's voice was tight with pleasure, and his body was, too. His thighs trembled already, and when Jace gently swiped his tongue across the opening, Charlie's whole body almost seized up.

"*Please!*"

"Please what?" Jace murmured, kissing a few times and

swiping his tongue around it again. He was working faster now, though, feeling the urgency burning through his own body. Fuck, he needed to get it in before *he* came, just from listening to, feeling, every single goddamn reaction Charlie had.

Every time they fucked, his own walls—stupid, self-imposed walls of how often he should fuck, and how, and who, and why—crumbled a little more.

It felt good. *So* fucking good. And making Charlie lose his mind with pleasure? Even better.

If being impulsive ended with his tongue pushing slowly into Charlie until Charlie was wet and gasping his name in syllables he couldn't even finish, well, Jace could stand a little more of that.

"I swear to fucking fuck, I will fucking..." Charlie yanked at his wrists futilely once more. "*Please* fuck me! I know you need it. I need you, baby. Hard and fast. Right now."

That tone—how in the hell could Jace ever say no to it? Not to mention Jace was so goddamn hard it hurt. His cock pressed into Charlie's leg, but that was not where he needed it.

He let go of Charlie's wrists and Charlie gripped the bedsheets on either side of his head, pushing his hips up into Jace as he scooted up the bed. Lube took just one or two swipes of his hand down his achingly hard shaft, and then he paused. "Without a condom—?"

"Still nobody but you," Charlie whispered, and there was something else in his voice.

"Me too." Jace didn't want to make him think about whatever that was, so he pressed another slow kiss between Charlie's shoulder blades.

The head of his cock easily slid into Charlie, and then the gorgeous man under him was taking every inch of him. Jace thrust slowly, a low groan escaping his throat. He couldn't explain how fucking good it felt to have Charlie wrapped around him, enveloping and squeezing, wet and needy...

"*Hard,*" Charlie reminded him in a growl, shoving his hips back into Jace.

Jace didn't need prompting again. His hands fell to Charlie's shoulders, pushing him face-down into the bed while Charlie rose up on his knees, pushing his ass up against Jace's groin.

Thrust after thrust, hard and fast, Jace felt his head spinning, his body tightening, Charlie's squirming under him intensifying, and he could hardly fucking stand to think the moment would end.

"Yes!" Charlie moaned, his voice muffled, his body shivering and clenching. He was trembling on the edge of ecstasy, flinching and pushing up again with every thrust of Jace's cock across his prostate.

*I can't stop myself needing him.*

Jace's last bit of control slipped away, and he pounded into him for those few last thrusts, exactly as they both needed him to.

"Yes! Baby! Fuck, Jace...!" Charlie was coming hard, squeezing around him, his muscles clenching and releasing as he rocked up and pushed into Jace's dick, taking him so fucking deep...

Jace couldn't hold it. He bit Charlie's shoulder as he came with a cry of his own—Charlie's name, no less. The blackness of utter focus on Charlie hit him again. His own cock was buried deep in Charlie's ass, pulsing with pleasure and wetness just like the ecstasy that tingled at his every nerve, the sweat from exertion that trickled down his chest and dampened his cheeks and hair.

"Oh, *fuck,* yes," Charlie moaned, reaching back to grab his hip with one hand, his forearm with the other. He rolled his head to the side and Jace pressed his nose against the back of Charlie's head, both of them collapsing to the bed with Jace still inside.

Jace pulled out slowly, cheeks flushing at how fucking hot Charlie looked—damp with both of their sweat, wetness trickling between his thighs, flushed red from head to toe, and best of all...

The far-away look on his face, like he still couldn't collect his wits.

"That..." Charlie managed, his voice trailing off as his chest heaved.

"Take your time," Jace laughed quietly, but honestly, he knew what Charlie meant. He was out of breath, out of energy, but how fucking *good* he felt. He only realized a minute or two later that he was still pressed against Charlie from chest to dick, their legs tangled, blanketing him against the bed.

When he rolled off, Charlie moaned quietly. "Jesus."

"Did I crush you?"

"No," Charlie breathed, then managed a quick laugh. "Fuck. I don't know. I don't care. That was so good."

He looked even more spacey than usual right now, his eyes still faraway, his lips tugging into a broad smile.

Jace grinned as he pushed himself up on an elbow and pressed a kiss to the back of his head. "Be right back."

"Mmhmm."

He rose to his feet and padded to the ensuite, taking a second to make sure his feet were steady under him first. His heart was still light, a smile tugging at his lips.

Jace brushed his teeth and gargled quickly, giving Charlie an extra minute of silence to recover from being teased to the very brink and held there for so long. When he was done, he finally looked out of the bathroom, only to see Charlie still lying there on his front, arms folded under his head.

"Want me to bring back a cloth?"

"Mmhmm." Charlie sounded as blissed-out as he had a minute ago, too.

"Water?"

"Mmhmm."

Jace quirked an eyebrow and looked over at him. "A sandwich?"

"Turkey."

Jace sighed as he came back from the bathroom, tossing a warm cloth at Charlie. Direct hit—right across that sexy little ass. He bent over to pull on underwear and jeans. "Damn. I didn't think you were listening."

Charlie beamed at him and finally moved, looking as boneless as he sounded, to wipe himself down. "For once, it paid to listen to you."

"Ohhh." Jace flipped Charlie off but grinned as he headed for the door.

"No crusts."

"You're kidding." Charlie gave him a look and rolled his eyes, so Jace just stared back at him. "You're not kidding. Ugh. First one thing, then another," he pretended to grumble, as if he weren't trying not to glow like the fucking sun right now.

Charlie just winked at him. "You want me letting you tease me again?" Oh, God, yes. The look on Jace's face must have given him away, because Charlie looked smug as he stretched, lazy and naked and *gorgeous* on Jace's bed. "The orgasm was great. Still hate you for that. No crusts."

"Hate you, too." Jace let his gaze wander down Charlie's body from head to toe and back up again.

*Or pretty damn near the opposite.*

He headed for the kitchen, before he could put his foot in his mouth for real.

When Charlie joined him in the kitchen, dressed and coherent again, he devoured the sandwich within minutes, and Jace did his best not to cuddle. They might have stood pretty close at the kitchen counter while they ate and talked about nothing in particular, but Jace wasn't counting.

It felt natural to show him properly around the place, so he did, and Charlie's eyes took in everything. Recovered from the amazing sex, apparently, Charlie was observant.

"That's a gorgeous art print."

Ah. Right. There *were* still a few things that reminded him of Mike—this piece, which they'd bought together at an art gallery the week he'd gotten the promotion to chief, for example.

"Thanks," Jace answered, his voice tight. "So, what are your plans this week, before the proposal?"

Charlie glanced at him but took the hint and explained his class and flight schedule that week while Jace nodded and took in the details.

Jace couldn't escape those last few ties to Mike, and he didn't want to... things like that piece were a part of his own past, not just their shared one. But it was also a pressing and rather unwelcome reminder of his own damn promise to himself.

However hot the sex, he was still technically a married man. The divorce wasn't finalized. And that sat with him about as well as ever.

Jace tuned back in, just in time to hear Charlie say, "I have family phone calls, too."

"Ugh. Good or bad?"

"Er... bit of both," Charlie admitted. "But I should head home and do that."

Jace tried to pretend he wasn't relieved. As intensely as he needed Charlie, he also needed space to figure out what the fuck they were doing. "Yeah. Of course."

The next time Charlie tried to go for a kiss, he was on his way out the door to take care of those unspecified family phone calls, and Jace couldn't help his flinch. He held steady for the actual kiss, but it was too late.

Charlie paused, drew back, and gazed at him for a moment. "You don't want me to stick around." It was a statement, not an offer or a question.

"I..." Jace trailed off, then cleared his throat and glanced away. "Not your fault, but no."

Charlie didn't look offended, though... just amused. Whatever was causing that, he kept it to himself as he pulled on his shoes. "I'm not letting you forget your promise."

"For...?" Jace blanked for a second, and then blushed at the look Charlie gave him. The sex. "Ah. Er, yeah. That."

How stupid an idea was it to have a boyfriend before he even got rid of Mike? What would he think? He knew he'd been divorced, but Jace was pretty sure he hadn't gotten into the nitty-gritty details yet, and that was pretty damn big.

Charlie's gaze flickered between Jace's eyes. "Shutting me out won't work, by the way. I'm an *expert* at it."

Jace's jaw tightened. It was hard to hear the words, even if they were directed at him without malice.

Mike had told him that, too—that he'd shut him out. And he had, sometimes in critical moments. Largely out of those stupid self-inflicted fears over how exactly his life was supposed to be set up... but also because he couldn't trust him.

But Charlie? He could trust him.

A spark of annoyance was still kindling in Jace's chest, and he pressed his lips together.

"I knew that would piss you off," Charlie added with a

carefree grin. "I'll give you time to think about it, but we're gonna see all our friends at the proposal this weekend."

Shit. He was right. Jace wasn't sure they *could* go back to acting like catty friends, or frenemies, or whatever the hell this had qualified as before *feelings* got into the mix.

Charlie's voice was soft. "So, think about it."

He paused as he pulled open the door, his gaze flickering down to Jace's lips. He didn't try for a goodbye kiss, and neither did Jace.

Whatever that conversation was, he needed more time to think about it. But the emotions that flooded Jace once the door was closed were clear.

Relief not to be put on the spot, but disappointment. Then, understanding: Charlie was making a point of not chasing him. He wanted him to be sure he wanted *him*, too.

And he did.

*I was never supposed to, and here I am.*

And the little piece of him that was convinced Charlie was going to let go and drift on, glide through life until he bumped into someone else at his own altitude... it pulled at his thoughts.

Jace sighed and went to grab a beer. It was going to be a long week.

2 0

———

CHARLIE

Charlie pushed the bar once more, keeping the wings level to ensure the smoothest possible landing as the ground rose to meet them. Landing on wheels was less exciting, less aesthetically beautiful, but far more accessible combined with a tow launch. It opened up gliding as a sport for people like Ash.

It had been a struggle to keep his excitement down, but at least it masqueraded as excitement for this flight—Ash's first, and he swore just before takeoff, last. He'd raised nearly a thousand dollars for his charity, which was probably the only reason he'd even gotten into the harness, swearing under his breath the whole time.

But, just as he'd expected, Ash had actually enjoyed himself when he was up in the air. It wasn't hard to feel the joy radiating from Ash as he observed the curve of the world, felt awe about being on the edge of space, admired the view up and down the California coastline.

Charlie figured takeoff and landing was still debatable, but before they were done with the flight, Ash was asking him about learning to go solo.

Jace, Liam, Dylan, Chris, two of Ash's mechanic course friends and Hannah were all there, rushing in once the glider had landed to greet them.

Once he was out of the harness and he'd helped Ash out, too, it was Charlie's job to detach the wing glider camera and turn it subtly toward Chris and Ash, watching Ash get his balance with his cane.

Charlie couldn't help his grin when Chris finally went down on a knee and Ash whispered a reverent, "Oh, my God."

"I know it's early, but I also know you're the one." Chris's voice was thick with emotion.

Charlie didn't look at Jace—couldn't look at him just now. They had texted a few times that week, but they hadn't seen each other, and he was fucking dying to know what Jace was thinking right now.

"I knew it was you from the second we met. I'm so damn proud of how far you've come, baby. And you still have so much to do. I want to be by your side every step of the way."

Ash was crying. Several of the other guys were wiping their cheeks in a manly fashion, except Dylan, who was delicately dabbing his eyes. But for his part, Charlie was grinning so hard it hurt.

Then, the big question.

"Will you marry me?"

"Yes."

Everyone was applauding now, but the two lovers were caught up in their own private moment. And then Charlie was glancing around at the others, and he made eye contact with Jace.

It was hard to tell what Jace was thinking, but he was smiling softly. He nodded once at Charlie, and Charlie lost track of time for a second.

*I'm ready to chase someone for a change.*

When they were finally pulling apart, Chris's grin spread even more. "And I have one more thing to say."

Charlie had missed the other one—oh, yeah. Flower girl. Sophie. Something about that. Jace's expression had swept him off to a whole different place there.

"What?" Ash looked up at Chris quickly, rubbing the new wedding band with his thumb.

"This is *totally* up to you... and we'll talk more about it before I ask for a yes or no. But we've planned Liam and Dylan's wedding so it could be a double wedding."

"What?" Dylan gasped, staring at Liam, who just beamed back at him. "Oh, my God. You kept that secret?"

Ash's eyes were watery but wide, his jaw dropping. "You'd do that?" His voice was low and... well, stunned with disbelief. "You'd marry me next week?"

"Babe, I'd marry you two months ago."

Ash's free hand was fisted in Chris's shirt like he might faint. "You'd... do that? You don't have to share your day," he finally managed to Dylan and Liam, but he was starting to smile.

"I'd love to," Dylan admitted, grinning at him. "But only if you don't want your own day."

Ash shook his head. "I don't have anyone to invite except... whoever's already here," he waved around at the group. "*Shit,* that's why you weren't asking me to do groomsman duties!"

Liam laughed and nodded.

"I... Fuck. Yes. If it's not, you know, a... hassle." Ash's nature wouldn't let him say otherwise, and they all knew it.

Chris grinned and pulled him in for another hug. "Hon. It's not. We planned it like this. I'm just glad you're not beating me off—"

"Oh, dirty," Liam snickered.

"—with your cane! *Dude.* Way to ruin the romantic moment."

They were all breaking up in laughter, though. Charlie grinned, keeping the camera as steady as he could. This was going to be one hell of a video.

"Yes. Yes, I want to," Ash breathed out. "I'll go get the license with you today if you want."

The look of stunned delight on Chris's face was adorable. "You will? Dude, that's a yes?"

"Dude," Ash teased, pulling him in for one more slow kiss before finishing, "it's a yes."

Charlie cleared his throat and blinked a few times, letting the applause settle again before shutting off the camcorder.

Then, Jace wandered closer to him. "Got that all on tape, huh? Clever."

"Wait 'til he realizes," Charlie chuckled quietly. "He and Dylan will wear the video file out from replaying it."

He let the others go first—the two happy couples, then Ash's friends, congratulating him. He left the glider pack-up to Hannah as he and Jace stepped to the side to oversee it.

"That was really sweet," Jace said after a moment, gazing after the group. "I gotta admit, I was nervous for Chris."

"That took balls," Charlie agreed. "Offering or accepting a proposal that fast. But they always say you'll know when it's the right person."

"It's true." Jace's tone made Charlie pause and glance at him. Acceptance, and a touch of sadness. *Shit. His ex.*

"I'm... sorry. I didn't mean to—" Charlie started.

Jace snorted. "Oh, don't start apologizing now. You'll harsh our... vibe."

"Harsh our vibe." Charlie bit his lip. "Groove our mellow?"

"I might not be down with the kids and their dating lingo

now," Jace warned, wagging his finger, "but I can tell when I'm being made fun of."

"Good." Charlie winked. "Gotta keep that clear."

"And it's part of my life. You're right. I was shutting you out from things that... um, I didn't think you'd like to hear." Jace drew a quick, deep breath. "So I'll try not to. You can talk about it, too. It's not that fresh—not anymore."

Charlie hummed, wandering closer to take care of the tow engine while Hannah broke down the rest of the glider. "Well... I figured it was a long-term monogamous kind of deal. The way you reacted to me at first."

Jace nodded once, but his eyes were guarded. Charlie paused to give him a second to realize, and then Jace did, his expression clearing. "Ah. Yes. On my side, it was."

"He cheated." Jace nodded once, and Charlie winced. "Sorry."

"It's all right. I had all the warning signs. It was repeated. It just took me a while to realize he wasn't stopping," Jace told him simply. "He's a good guy, but he has addictions, and he can't live with himself unless he's seducing men. Groups, usually. Fine for him, but it's not... *my* scene."

Charlie pressed his lips together and nodded. "Is that why you got hot and cold on me?"

"Mm... mostly." Jace nodded toward the fenceline. Someone was trying to get their attention.

"What?" Charlie yelled back, almost annoyed at the interruption.

Liam cupped his hands around his mouth and tried again. That projection worked. "Supper. Come with us."

Dinner sounded great. "Will do!" Charlie shouted, then held up ten fingers in the air.

Jace saluted. "I'll find out what restaurant it is and text you. See you soon, yeah?"

"Save me a seat," Charlie told Jace.

And Jace just smiled at him, then leaned in slightly. "Can I?"

Charlie didn't bother to look if anyone was looking. It didn't matter. He wanted Jace either way. "Yeah."

They pressed their lips together, slow and sweet. The day had settled into Charlie's bones, and he didn't feel a rush to do, say, *be* anything at all. It couldn't get better now, especially with Jace's hand cupping his cheek.

When Jace finally pulled back, Charlie was grinning like a damn fool, and he didn't care about that, either. "See you."

To her credit, Hannah waited until Jace was almost out of earshot before she shoved the glider into the car and hissed, "*Dude*! You have a motherfucking hot-as-shit firefighting captain boyfriend with muscles on his muscles, and you didn't tell me?!"

Charlie's cheeks heated up. "Must have slipped my mind. Coming to dinner?"

"You think they'll mind?"

"Nah. You'll wanna get to know Ash anyway. He wants to fly solo."

Hannah pumped her fist. "Yes. He's our brand of crazy. And your boyfriend?"

"Don't—not yet."

"Uh huh. And the guy who wants to be your boyfriend?" Hannah followed up without missing a beat.

Charlie's cheeks flushed. His phone went off with a text from Jace—the restaurant name and a simple *xox*. He looked up at her. "I don't know, yet, that..."

Hannah gave him a look. "We all saw the way he looks at you."

Charlie strode for the driver's side of the car. "All packed up? Good."

"You're my ride. You can't escape me."

"Damn."

But Charlie was flushed with pleasure and pride. Hang-gliding hangovers were real, but he couldn't remember the last time he'd felt so acutely like he was two thousand feet in the air, all with his feet on solid ground.

## JACE

It was a miracle they'd managed to avoid the subject.

Through quick conversational escape routes, the general chaos of the final elements that had to fall into place for the double wedding, and the discretion of their friends, nobody questioned Jace and Charlie on their relationship status.

Which suited Jace perfectly, because most of the time he didn't spend talking to his guys at the firehouses, at the therapist, or arranging wedding details, he was in Charlie's bed or vice versa.

Charlie's schedule was slow at this time of year, and Jace was due back at work the day after tomorrow. They wanted to make the most of it. His family seemed to have decided that the wedding took priority this year and were off his back; at this time of December, nobody was organizing social get-togethers.

So it wasn't until the champagne started flowing at the reception that they found themselves under the spotlight.

"Soooo," Chris drawled, wandering closer to the table where he and Charlie were sitting, drinking their way through a bottle and making fun of their friends' dancing. Ash was busy gossiping with Dylan, and Liam was retelling some kind of story to the groomsmen.

Charlie swapped looks with Jace. "Uh oh. Here's trouble."

"Damn straight," Jace agreed.

Chris wagged a finger and pulled out a chair, then turned it backward and sat on it. He folded his arms across the back. "Actually, I'm bi."

"Hi, Bi. I'm Charlie—Charles!" But Charlie's correction came a second too late.

A grin tugged at Jace's lips while Chris laughed. "Charlie-Charles, huh?"

"*You* shut up."

"Or what?" Jace teased, leaning in. "You'll make me?"

Charlie looked straight at him, then stuck out his tongue. "Maybe I will."

It was all Jace could do not to kiss him. He turned to grab his glass and sipped again instead. *Calm down, there, cowboy,* he advised himself.

But when he looked at Chris, his employee and their friend looked stunned. Jace couldn't blame him. He didn't usually get like *this* in public. He'd only had a glass or two of bubbly, so he couldn't even blame that.

It was fucking completely Charlie's fault.

Jace was high off him. He couldn't get enough time with him, and even at the wedding, spending that whole day not holding hands, only sneaking kisses when they were alone together, so as not to lead people into thinking they were together... it was fucking hard.

But he wasn't ready for the conversation yet—not the big D one. Only the little D one. And it wasn't just his dick involved. It hadn't been for a couple weeks now, honestly.

Chris sounded thoughtful now, his gaze sliding between

them. "Hm. So you're in that awkward in-between. Sort that shit out, guys."

"Thanks for the advice," Charlie muttered, rolling his eyes.

Chris countered with a wink. "I think it's my prerogative. Listen to the newlywed. Look, man. Even with Mike, you've never been like *this*. It looks good on you. That's all." He held up his hands. "No more meddling."

"No more," Jace repeated with a skeptical eyebrow raise.

Chris winked and rose to his feet. "Maybe a little more, if you take *too* long about it."

"Thanks." But Jace was laughing despite himself. Chris cared—he really did—and Jace heard what he was saying, because it was exactly what he'd been thinking just moments ago, and all week long.

There was something about Charlie.

Once Chris left, they were alone together again, tucked away at this table out of the way of the dance floor and the bar and anywhere else people were congregating.

"So," Jace spoke up, rolling his eyes, "everyone knows."

"They do. You okay with that?" Charlie asked, his expression fading to a serious one at last.

Jace caught his breath. Honestly, he wasn't sure. He'd been afraid first, of what people would think of him dating so soon after the divorce. And of his own recklessness, wondering what counted as a rebound.

But Charlie was the right guy.

So he deserved to know.

Jace finished his glass of champagne and drew a breath, turning to face Charlie. "The divorce is still recent. The breakup was a long time ago. The *official* breakup was a few months ago."

Charlie nodded seriously. "And by the divorce being recent...?"

It was hard to get the words out. "It's not finalized." Jace kept his voice low. "California law. It's filed, and then you have to wait six months before you're technically single. That period started just over a month ago."

Charlie visibly reeled, setting aside his glass and folding his arms. "Right when we met."

Jace tried not to make his smile bitter. *Now* Charlie understood his hesitation. "On a Thursday. We met on a Sunday."

"Wow."

"Yeah." Jace looked away, over the sea of happy people. Liam had a lot of friends, and so did Chris. There were family members, too, and even Dylan's weird mom had shown up. No evil exes to interrupt the ceremony, either. It had been pretty much perfect.

He hoped he wasn't going to ruin the mood—for Charlie, at least.

"It must feel like you're trapped."

Jace hadn't expected that reaction, or the truth of it to burn a hole in the knot of worry in his chest.

Ouch.

"Yeah," Jace managed, clearing his throat for a moment and looking back at him. "Yeah, actually. I've been... well, the first divorce papers were served a couple months ago now, and we saw it coming for a long time—a couple years, at least—before then. But it's like it never ends."

Charlie took his hand and squeezed lightly. "So, five more months. That's nothing compared to all the time you had to wait to be free."

"You're supposed to be pissed off at me," Jace objected. "Not being smart about this."

Charlie laughed. "Hey. I'm blindsided, don't get me wrong. But it's not like we've agreed to elope tomorrow."

"No. Jesus, no," Jace almost fell over himself to answer,

grabbing Charlie's hand. "I don't want that to sound like I'm coming on too quickly—"

"Shh." Charlie leaned in across the table and pressed a quiet kiss to his lips. "Stop worrying, Cannon."

The sexy nickname made Jace's cheeks flush, but it had the intended effect of distracting him from his worries for a moment.

"I don't know how to react to the news yet, and we haven't even talked about whether we're ready for relationships," Charlie told him.

"Exactly," Jace murmured. The idea that Charlie might not want one, after all this time Jace had taken to decide he was ready...

Jace's heart was vulnerable right now. He couldn't afford to have it broken again.

"But I like you. You like me. We'll figure it out." Charlie finally let go of his hand and grabbed their glasses. It wasn't a direct answer, but it wasn't clearly pissed off at him for not explaining until now, either. Very mature. Jace liked that. "For tonight," Charlie reminded him, "we have four very happy men to toast. So I'm going to the bar to continue that. I'll need more champagne to handle all this cleanup duty."

"Yeah." Jace cleared his throat and picked up his phone. "I'll make sure their cars are still ready for pickup."

Charlie's hand affectionately slid across his shoulder. "Is that on the list?" he teased.

"I'll show you a list," Jace threatened idly, scrolling through his phone.

"Nah. I'll let you handle that. Sounds boring, like work." Charlie winked and sauntered off. Jace's eyes fell to that sexy little ass and the way his trousers clung to it.

God, it suddenly *did* sound like work... but the prize?

Totally worth it.

2 2

CHARLIE

"Charles, could I trouble you for a word?"

Before Jenny even finished speaking, Charles's heart sank. He put his feet up on the coffee table and gripped the phone a little harder. No matter how incredible the wedding yesterday had been, and how well work had gone that morning, that phone call was never good. Especially not right before Christmas.

"Sure. Of course. I know it's going to cost more to have him on increased nursing support," Charlie answered, not wanting to drag this out. "The billing department's going to be in touch soon, right?"

Jenny's sigh of relief was audible. "Yeah. Thank you for being understanding about it."

The way Charlie saw it, he didn't really have a choice. His dad had more bad days than good days now, but he was happy here. There was no way he could just uproot him to a cheaper place, and no way he could trust that they'd actually take care of him there.

But he also didn't have extra money to throw at them. It

was going to be a couple hundred extra a month, easy. He made rent, he never fell behind on bills, but he also wasn't saving for retirement already. There was no more in his life that he could rearrange without starting to compromise his quality of life.

Not without moving in with someone, anyway.

He brushed that thought *firmly* away. Moving in with someone for financial reasons alone was a disaster waiting to happen. It was time to earn more money.

Or call his siblings up, but his sister already paid half of Dad's fees. And she didn't have any time to spare. His little brother, though? Brian gave them a hundred bucks here or there for gifts for Dad, and he never visited. No wonder. He wouldn't take a job to save his life.

Maybe it was time to whip Brian into shape. His dad hadn't been able to, but between him and his sister...

Once he finished the small talk with Jenny, assuring her that he'd be over later that day to see his dad for the residents' gift swap, he hung up. Then, he waited long enough to calm down so he'd have the patience to keep pressing redial until Brian picked up.

"Hey, bro."

Charlie *did* love Brian despite his flakiness—his unwillingness to deal with anything at all related to this situation—so he didn't launch on the offensive. "Hey, man. Long time without hearing from you."

"Yeah, yeah. Life's been great. Crazy but good."

Charlie paused, wondering if he wanted to know. If people thought *he* was an irresponsible drifter for his career choices, Brian was a whack job. "Oh?"

"Been on a road trip, man. Went up and down the coast. Played in my new little acoustic band, hit up little beach bars on the coast. We're doing great!"

Charlie rubbed his eyes. "And Paul... he's still keeping the profits, huh?"

"How'd you know?"

"Lucky guess." Charlie was pretty sure Paul was drinking away the money, not reinvesting it in advertising, but Brian would hear none of it.

It was frustrating. Brian was smart, when he wasn't high or listening to those guys' stupid ideas. He *could* do better.

"And that girl?"

"Oh, man. I don't even know which one you mean," Brian admitted.

Charlie wasn't surprised. "It's like that, huh? Still nobody?"

"No, man. Nobody to tie me down. Speaking of which, what about you? Not grounded yet, huh?"

"No, still flight lessons. I'm looking at ramping up my business real soon, actually," Charlie told him. "I need to, which is why I'm calling you."

"You know I don't know much about business *or* hang-gliding," Brian chuckled nervously. He'd heard the sound of bills.

Charlie kicked back on his couch with a can of soda, pressing it to his forehead. *Stay cool.* "No, but you do know what's up with Dad. You never called back."

"Yeah. Things got busy. That sounds rough."

"But the bright side... if you don't have anyone to visit for Christmas..." Charlie hinted strongly. "I don't know if I can this year, again."

He'd gone to spend the day with his dad every year for, God, six years now? With Justin by his side, then alone. It got harder every year.

"What? What about Jemma?"

"You know the kids don't like seeing their granddad like that," Charlie said quietly. "And she sends money."

There was a moment's silence.

Charlie pressed it. "Man, I know you don't have a career, and—you have the music thing developing, but you can't live like that forever. *I* can't take all this on myself forever. It'll help both of us out if you can figure something out, you know? If you can't chip in financially, you live in the same damn city." Or close, anyway, last he'd heard. "You can come see him more. It'll make him really happy, Brian. And it'll help me. I don't have time to see him, and work, and..."

"And?" Brian chose to focus on that, not the rest of the message.

"Date, or start a family, or whatever's next."

Brian's tone was noncommittal, at best. "I don't know if I'll ever afford a family. But that's the choice I've made."

"Then come see him for Christmas, at least. Jenny just told me the fees are going up."

"Again," Brian muttered.

*Not like you started chipping in last time I told you they were going up.* Charlie held his tongue, though. Saying that wouldn't help anything. Then it struck him that he was being remarkably restrained and diplomatic.

Maybe someone was rubbing off on him a little. His heart hurt.

"Yeah," Charlie decided to go with. "So something has to give. It's been my personal life for so long."

*And it's going to have to be again. I can't stop seeing him, if neither of my siblings will. And I can't work less, if they can't pay more.*

He rested his head against the back of the couch. "Anyway, I won't keep you."

"Yeah, got practice to get to," Brian told him, suddenly all business. "And Christmas dinner with some of the guys, doing a potluck."

Charlie's heart sank. "Yeah. Cool. Have fun. Call me more."

"I will. Bye."

Charlie hung up and muttered, "You won't." He tossed his phone on the couch next to him, then noticed the message alert and picked it back up.

*Recovered from the party last night? Wanna come over tonight?*

It was Jace, of course.

Charlie didn't know how to broach the subject. While Jace had been trying to put off his work, rearrange his schedule around Charlie's lower availability, there was a whole new kettle of fish he hadn't devoted thought to.

Hearing last night that the man was still married had been... not a shock, but a surprise, at least. He'd been upfront about why and how—the details hadn't really changed from what Charlie had known before—but still.

*Was* he just a rebound? Was Jace using him to get back at Mike somehow? Was he just exploring sexually with him now that he had a taste of freedom?

Charlie knew there was more to it than that, but it was another small stress on this pile of stressors.

And it reminded him that relationships were tough on him. They always had been. If he was with Jace—really with him— there was no dilly-dallying around. Jace was all or nothing, black or white. It had clearly been a struggle for him even not to get an answer to their conversation at the reception last night.

Charlie couldn't take it slow with this man. They hadn't, to date, and that wasn't going to change.

But rushing headlong into a relationship, and figuring out his responsibilities to his family, and expanding his business? All at once? That was a recipe for disaster.

He picked up and put down the phone a few times before he started to type out a response.

*I'm on my way to see my dad.*

It wasn't shooting him down, but it certainly wasn't a warm and friendly invitation to come over, either.

Jace's response was forthright and simple, as usual.

*Do you need time to think about what I told you?*

Well, if he put it like that.

*Yeah. I have a lot of commitments right now. God knows I'm allergic to them.*

*You commit really well to what you're passionate about. I like that about you. But it's up to you.*

Charlie half-smiled, rubbed his face, and pocketed his phone. He wasn't going to get carried away on compliments.

Maybe he could commit well—reluctantly, but deeply—but that didn't mean he *should*. Not necessarily.

Charlie's first responsibility was to his family, wasn't it? That meant, as always, relationships had to go on the back burner. And Jace had to wait until he was divorced before he was technically available, right?

He grabbed lunch before he hit the road for Pine Grove.

It wasn't avoidance.

## JACE

"Fuck."

Jace didn't get an answer to his text, and he was pretty damn sure he knew why.

If he'd been running before, it was Charlie running now.

He'd taken too long to tell him about the divorce. Or to tell him that he wanted him, for real. Or Charlie was just over him now, looking for someone who was less rigid. Or he was committing too fast, and scaring Charlie off.

Realistically, he knew better. He'd made a hell of a bad marriage work for too many years by knowing better. But what was he supposed to do when he offered Charlie space and Charlie ran?

When his phone rang, he didn't expect it to be Liam.

"Hey. Is everything all right for the newlyweds?" he greeted.

"Great. Couldn't be better," Liam assured him, which made his heart sink even further.

But Jace kept a smile fixed on his lips so his mood didn't carry over to the phone. "Oh, phew. I thought the car dropped you off in the brush or something. Wild camping: the new honeymoon trend."

Liam laughed richly. "God, Dylan's face if I brought him—yeah, no, honey. Don't worry about it," he said to Dylan in the background. "No," he said into the phone again. "Chris and Ash came over, and we were all just talking about yesterday. So we wanted to say thanks to you and Charlie for all you did for us."

"Of course, man. It was great. I was glad to help," Jace said, and that much was the truth. It had kept him focused on everything until now, when he was starting the job again tomorrow and... well, pretty scared of it.

No anxiety attacks since the office Christmas party, either. He put that down to therapy and Charlie's presence.

"So, you and Charlie, huh? Chris was telling me."

Jace groaned quietly. "Don't let me ruin the mood, man. It's your first day of being married."

"No way. If this is relationship advice time, I'm out. Hold on."

"No, I—"

"You're on speakerphone. Say hi!"

The chorus of *hellos* and *heys* from the other three guys made Jace smile for a moment.

"Congrats again, guys," Jace answered them all. "But seriously, get busy celebrating."

Chris snickered. "Oh, we have been. We need a break every now and then, though. Tell us what's up with Charlie."

"Uh." Jace stalled for a moment, then gave in. "Basically... I told him about the divorce, and now he's kind of backing off."

"He's allergic to commitments, isn't he?" Ash pointed out. "I know that much."

"Yeah. So I figured maybe I came on too strong."

Dylan snickered. "Catching the bouquet and giving it to him may have been a clue."

"Yeahhh." Jace winced. "*Anyway*, he's avoiding me today. So I'm deciding whether to give him space, that kind of thing."

"You like him. Chase him. Tell him that. I don't think he'll believe it unless he hears it from you," Ash said simply.

Liam added, "If your heart's already in this, what have you got to lose?"

There were a few moments of silence.

"Jesus, that's deep," Chris laughed. "You should see the look Dylan's giving him right now."

Jace laughed, too, but his heart was racing. Fuck. Liam was *right*. He had to at least find out what was wrong. "I'll leave you all to it, then."

"You're going to see him, right?"

Jace rubbed his forehead, ignoring the nerves that coiled in his stomach.

He couldn't get away with pretending they didn't like each other forever. Sooner or later, he had to admit that his heart *was* on the line again. He'd never meant it to be, but...

Things happened.

"Yeah. Thanks. Anyway, it was a pleasure helping you out yesterday. Enjoy."

After the chorus of goodbyes, Jace smiled at his phone.

He did have friends still, and they were sensible. Discreet enough not to push him about it, but insightful, too.

They saw his heart getting involved before he'd even realized the extent of it. And they weren't trying to wrap him in bubblewrap, either.

So, just like Chris had said, they saw something between the two of them that was worth fighting for. The same thing Jace felt—the same thing that had pulled him along toward him, despite his promises to himself not to get involved too fast.

His mind was made up. He grabbed his car keys and sent a text.

*Pine Grove, right? I'll be in the parking lot in 15 minutes. If you can't talk yet, it's okay. Hugs available too.*

---

Jace had barely found a parking spot and climbed out of the car when he spotted Charlie.

It wasn't hard to see him—a bright red ugly Christmas sweater, flushed cheeks, and a quick pace that wasn't quite a run, but almost.

Charlie wasn't having a good day. Jace could tell by the set of his shoulders and mouth. He just held out his arms wide, and when Charlie crashed against his chest, he squeezed him as hard as he could.

"Thank you," Charlie breathed out. "Fuck. My brain's been a mess. I'm sorry I tried to ditch you..."

"You have every right to, if you need time to think. But I felt like you needed a friend today, at least," Jace murmured back, holding Charlie tightly against his chest. They swayed gently in that way people did when they hugged for a long time.

"Yeah. God, yeah," Charlie murmured after a few moments. "And really, I already know... I just didn't want to say over the phone."

"Go for it." Jace tried to hide the nervousness that flashed through his body, the fear that Charlie was about to let him down easily.

"I don't think I'm a good boyfriend." Charlie was so fucking blunt about it that it made Jace hurt on his behalf. "And I'm in a bad place. I have... I have to start working a lot more, to pay for," he gestured silently behind him to the building.

Although his words sounded foreboding, his expression was open and... pained. It was hurting him to say it.

*His heart's on the line, too.*

"So you want to focus on your career."

"Yeah. No. I don't *want to*," Charlie murmured, "but I have to."

"So do I," Jace told him softly. "It's going to take a long time and a lot of work before my guys trust me at work. That doesn't mean we can't try *something* out between us."

Charlie hesitated, his brows drawing together. "But you haven't even met my family."

"So? I know *you*. I l—I like you." *Shit. Wow. That word came too easily.*

Love. He did love him.

Shit, this was a bad time to realize it, in the parking lot of a retirement home, his arms looped around the waist of a man who was pulling back in every way but physically.

"Oh." Charlie looked stunned for a moment. "Even...? But I'm. I'm..." he trailed off.

Jace laughed under his breath. "I don't think I deserve a good boyfriend, either. Or that I'd be one."

"No, you're—"

"You think I'm too good for you? And I think you're too good for me? Is that what we're both about to say?" Jace managed to crack a grin as he said it, and he wrung one from Charlie, too. "Hon. That's not how this works."

"You'd know, I guess," Charlie murmured, but it wasn't laced with the fiery, bitter accusation it might have been from someone else. Someone like Mike—or, he was willing to bet, Justin. It was simple fact.

"And you're okay with that?"

Charlie managed a little smile. "You told me, in your own

way, at the very start. I tried to be mad about it, but I can't be. There's... You haven't done anything wrong."

"Nor have you," Jace murmured, rubbing Charlie's back gently. "You play the free spirit, but you're trying to make everyone around you happy, too."

Charlie leaned into him again, pressing his face into his chest. Jace held him tightly as Charlie managed a quiet, "Yeah. I'm sorry I'm such a wreck today, Jesus. Just..."

"Being here isn't easy," Jace supplied.

Charlie nodded, and Jace gave him a minute. When Charlie straightened up again, looking a little clearer-headed, Jace offered him a quick smile.

"So, what do you need?"

Charlie instantly looked back at the building. "I know it's asking a lot, but..."

"I'll come in with you."

"You would? But my dad doesn't know you. He might never..." There it was. Charlie stopped in the middle of his sentence, the words hanging between them, his mouth open a little. Jace barely dared to breathe until Charlie filed away that revelation and finished, "Anyway, you wouldn't mind?"

*Crap. Of course. Why didn't I think of that?*

Jace knew well why not. He had his own family—distant, not great, but also not terrible. They could go holidays without seeing each other. Not the kind of bond Charlie had with his dad, or at least, wished he still had.

"Of course I wouldn't," Jace told him firmly.

Charlie looked down at the ground, and then his warm hand was sliding into Jace's. "And, even though I'm not sure I can... you know, *do* this... You wouldn't mind if we try?"

Jace could hardly find the words to say *yes*, and *no*, and *of course I wouldn't mind*, all at once. He couldn't remember which were the right ones. Crap. He didn't want to give the opposite answer...

But his face must have said it all, because Charlie laughed lightly for the first time since he'd come running out of the building for him, and pulled him in with a hand on his cheek for a quiet kiss. "I take that as a *go ahead*."

Jace cleared his throat. "Yeah. Yeah, we can try."

It wasn't enough for him, but what he needed was too much for Charlie.

Somewhere in the space in the middle lay the answer, and for the first time, he found himself willing to raise his head from the narrow path in front of him to look into the future.

A future with Charlie was worth a try.

2 4

---

CHARLIE

"I brought someone to see you, Dad."

In the back of his mind somewhere, Charlie had been waiting for this moment for years.

And Jenny's words the other day couldn't have come at a better time. Dad wouldn't want him to hold back his life, it was true. When he asked about Justin, it wasn't to see *Justin*. It was because he thought Justin made Charlie happy.

*He didn't, but Jace does.*

"And who's this?"

Before he'd gone to find Jace in the parking lot, it looked like his dad had been having a pretty good day. He prayed it kept up.

Before he or Jace could answer, though, his dad nodded. "Justin? You've changed!"

Jace paused and looked at Charlie.

"No, Dad. His name's Jace. I'm... seeing him, right now."

"Oh. Oh, all right." His dad squinted toward Jace, then waved him over. "Come here, then."

Jace walked over, his back straight and eyes focused. He

was keeping Charlie in his peripheral vision for cues, but he smiled, too.

"Pleasure to meet you, sir." Tall, handsome, charming... Jace was the perfect guy to introduce to your dad. Charles blushed as he thought it, watching them shake hands.

"You're seeing my Charles? What happened to that Justin guy?"

"He's... He left a few years back, Dad," Charlie said quietly.

"Well, why didn't you tell me?" Then, his dad looked worried. "Did you?"

"No, no," Charlie rushed to assure him. "I, uh. You liked him, and all."

"Well, you like this guy better, don't you? Course you do. Look at you. You're smiling around him."

Charlie flinched and nodded, his gaze drawn to the floor for a moment. Maybe his dad had seen more than he'd thought. But if so...

"Why... Didn't you like him?"

"I always liked keeping an eye on him," his dad told him, his jaw firm. "He didn't get you into any trouble, did he? He was a smooth talker, that one."

It was like a dam had burst in Charlie's chest.

"Charlie?" Jace murmured when Charlie was silent for a minute.

Charlie cleared his throat from the lump in it, drew a deep breath, and shook his head. "Nah. But he's better off gone."

"Course he is, because you've got... Jace, was it? Short for anything?"

"Jason Williams, sir."

Charlie reeled. "It is?"

Jace grimaced at him. "I never liked that name. Jason is my dad."

"Jace it is," Dad told him, leaning back in his chair. "You should have brought him earlier, Charles. Charlie? Is that what you're going by now? Justin used to say that. I never thought you liked it."

Charlie had his lips pressed together tightly to keep his emotions in check. "No, I didn't. I do now."

Jace cast him a soft, apologetic look, and Charlie shook his head. He hadn't been supposed to know.

"Well, I'll let you boys go. It's nearly dinnertime. They like to take extra time to fuss over me now," Charlie's dad finally said, looking back and forth between the two of them.

"Real pleasure meeting you, sir," Jace murmured with a nod toward him.

"You, too, son. Don't be a stranger."

Charlie leaned in to hug his dad tightly for a moment. "Thanks for not scaring him off."

"I'll work on it next time," his dad promised, patting his back lightly. "Get on going, while there's day still left. Enjoy yourselves while you're young."

Charlie looped his arm around Jace's and nodded jerkily. "Love you, Dad."

"You too, kid."

He made it almost all the way to the parking lot before the tears spilled out of his eyes, but when he made it to his car, Jace stopped him in his tracks and wrapped his arms around him again.

The solid wall of muscle around him kept him safe, helped him reel in his emotions until he could think straight.

"Are you okay to drive?"

"Yeah," Charlie murmured. "Can you follow my car?"

"Wherever you lead."

Jace let go and patted his cheek, then nodded briskly and strode off toward his own car, leaving Charlie looking after him.

*How did I get so damn lucky?*

It wasn't until they were pulling into Charlie's driveway that he realized the metaphor he'd been living out. He'd been checking his rearview mirror the whole time, making sure Jace was following.

Charlie put that thought aside, along with so many others, as he climbed out of the car and led the way inside.

"You're looking pretty tired," Jace told him. "I can make something to eat."

"Would you?" Charlie moaned. "I owe you big time."

"Nope. Only a little time." Jace pecked his lips once their shoes were off. "Let's see what you've got."

Charlie settled at the kitchen counter, smiling to himself at how strange it was to have someone in his kitchen and cooking for him. He could get used to this part, too.

There was a lot he could get used to with Jace around.

Jace settled on some kind of chicken-rice bake, and Charlie was perfectly happy with that choice. He chatted with Jace, showing him where the dishes were when needed, and otherwise staying out of his way.

After he finished describing his work day, a thought occurred to Charlie. "Oh, you're working again tomorrow, aren't you?"

"Yep. First day back," Jace murmured, a frown line appearing between his brows.

"It'll go well."

"Mmm." Jace clearly wasn't in the mood to talk about it, and Charlie understood that nervousness. He changed the subject to sports while they waited for the casserole to bake.

Turned out Jace was a damn good cook, too. Charlie

shouldn't have been surprised. He found himself learning about Napa valley wines while washing dishes alongside the man, and suddenly, the vague idea of moving in with someone to split costs didn't sound *that* bad.

Once the kitchen was tidy, Jace eyed him, then nodded toward the bedroom. "You should rest. You still look tired. Do you want me to stay?"

"Please do." Charlie reached for Jace's hand, lacing their fingers as naturally as breathing now. "Hell, take the spare key, come back after work. If you want?"

"Of course I want to." Jace tugged him along to his bedroom, ushering him to the bed and closing the door after them.

God, the way he moved was tidy. It made Charlie want to wring that animalistic lust out of him again, but maybe not tonight.

Soon, he promised himself. As soon as he made his mind up on what they were.

Wrapping himself around Jace's body was easy. Pressing his face into Jace's chest while Jace slid his arms around him and shifted their weight so neither of them would go numb was easy. Letting his breathing sync up with Jace's was easy.

That voice in the back of his head telling him that relationships were too much for him, that even Jace would leave sooner or later? That was hard to deal with.

His dad liked Jace, at least. But that brought him back to thinking about money, and about family, and how he was going to wind up crying alone in the parking lot on Christmas if it happened to be a bad day for his dad. Again.

It made the itch strengthen under his skin—the need to push himself until the pressure bled out, one way or another, by knife or glider or ice-cold shower or *something* that would break the numbness...

Charlie hadn't done one of those things in years, but he still wanted to. Especially on a day like today, when it felt like there were no right choices.

His breath caught in his throat, and he focused his thoughts on inhaling and exhaling, counting the breaths.

*If I can hold out for a night, I can hold out for more. Just one night.*

## 25

JACE

The call came at five AM—two hours before he was supposed to start his first shift.

But it didn't come from one of the crews, or the fire inspector, or even his boss. It was the hospital calling.

*Has there been a mistake?* Jace could feel Charlie's weight by him, warm and solid and reassuring, so he wasn't panicking. Who else would have his number?

He eased out of bed and grabbed the phone, keeping his voice down as he answered. Charlie hadn't stirred, and he didn't want to wake him. With everything on his mind, the poor guy could use the rest.

"Hello?"

"Mr. Williams? Jace Williams?"

"Yeah, that's me." Jace hopped into his underwear and jeans, then let himself out of the bedroom. "Who's in the hospital?"

"You're listed as the next-of-kin emergency contact for a Mike Williams."

"Gregory," he automatically corrected, then winced. "Mike Gregory now."

"My apologies."

"No. No, it's okay. Uh, is he at emergency?" Jace slipped back into the bedroom to grab his shirt and sweater. Charlie still hadn't budged, so getting out the door was a thirty-second deal. "I'm on my way."

"Yes, he is. He's in stable condition. We can give you further information when you arrive."

Jace had expected no less.

---

"It's two days before Christmas. What the fuck were you thinking?"

Jace hadn't expected to see Mike again, let alone attached to an IV and heart monitor, pale and prone in a hospital bed. Given the circumstances, he figured a little anger was justifiable.

"I wasn't." Mike's eyes were closed. He knew him by his footsteps alone, and knowing him, he didn't want to look Jace in the eye.

Jace knew better. He knew it was an addiction, that his neural pathways were literally hardwired to need the drugs, and knew he only did it because his self-esteem and his life had gone to shit.

But holy fuck, ODing wasn't like him.

"Mike. Was it a mistake?" Jace sank into the chair next to Mike's bed.

"Yes." Mike answered fast, and he opened his eyes, wincing but making eye contact. "Yeah. It was."

Jace believed him. He sighed and slumped over, elbows on his knees, chin on his fists. "There's nothing I can do."

"Yeah, there is. You..." Mike trailed off, then cleared his throat. "I just miss you."

"I'm not—we can't be friends. Not yet, at least," Jace murmured. "Not when you lied to me, over and over."

Mike sighed, the sound heavy with frustration. "It's the drugs, it—"

"I knew you were an addict for a long time. I've been by your side for all of it," Jace told him. "That wasn't the problem. It was the lies."

Mike was quiet for a minute before he nodded. "Ah. I guess... right."

Jace looked him in the eye again, slowly straightening up. "You could've asked to sleep with other guys."

Mike raised his eyebrow. "Would you have said yes?"

"Probably not. But we could have talked through it like adults. I don't know, maybe come up with something. But it wasn't about sex, was it?"

Mike slowly shook his head, hanging on Jace's every word.

*He expects me to fix his life for him... again.* Jace caught his breath as he realized what Mike was waiting for. *And take him back.*

As much as it hurt, as much as Mike needed someone, Jace couldn't fill that need. Well, he *could*... but not without neglecting himself.

Jace rose to his feet, shoving his hands into his pockets so he didn't take Mike's. "I loved you for a long time," he told Mike, keeping his voice as quiet as he could. "I still care about you. I don't want you ODing behind some trick's house. That's... You deserve better."

Mike had to look away, and Jace gave him a moment before his ex-husband looked back at him. "So did you. I'm... glad you did it. We did it."

"What? The marriage or the divorce?"

"Both," Mike said quietly.

Jace half-smiled. He knew what Mike meant. They'd had a good time together while it had lasted. Mike's decisions to sabotage it all were down to him, and if he got his act together, he could fix it himself, too.

There was a lot to love about Mike, even if Jace's trust or respect would never recover. Someone else would find him.

Just like someone had found Jace.

Mike cleared his throat. "Have you met someone? You look... different."

There wasn't a real point in lying—not after all this—so Jace nodded slowly. "Didn't really mean to. Didn't even like him, at first."

Mike cracked a grin. He knew Jace's temperament, and that he didn't suffer fools. "I'd like to have seen that."

Jace laughed softly. "Yeah. He's quite something." He refocused on Mike, finally reaching out to rest a hand on Mike's arm. "So are you, once you get through everything you're doing to sabotage yourself."

Mike's smile faded and he gritted his teeth, then nodded slightly.

"Take this as a wake up call. And take me off your damn emergency contacts." Jace's voice cracked and he cleared his throat, pulling his hand away and giving Mike a brisk nod.

"Yeah. I will. Thanks for... being here." Mike paused, then added, "I hope he makes you happy."

"Thanks. I hope *you* make you happy," Jace told Mike, raising a hand slightly.

He couldn't leave the hospital room fast enough after that, and the beginning of his shift was more than fucking welcome. For the first time in ages when thinking about his first day back, his anxiety was calm.

Compared to a relationship, give him a burning building any day.

---

"Unit three, respond."

Jace leaned on the side of the engine, his eyes intent on the ground. The fire was small, but intense—Christmas holidays always brought the weird ones. Someone had managed to explode a propane tank in their house.

Though everyone was out safely, there was a unit inside with a supply line. It wasn't a risk. They were close to an exit, conditions were great. The fire was dwindling on its own. But he couldn't stop checking on them.

"Copy that," Pete answered. "Working our way along side B. C's looking pretty hot, though, Chief."

"Is it still inside the walls?"

"Roger. It might be in the attic now."

Jace didn't hit the mic, but he smacked the side of the engine. "Damn it." These flimsy new-build houses melted like cotton candy on the tongue. Give him a good, solid brick house any day.

Kevin, the crew's engineer, clapped his shoulder. "Can't save 'em all. That's what insurance is for."

He was right. God knew Jace, of all people, was aware that a building wasn't worth any risk.

But it felt like conceding defeat to the beast he'd dreaded for so many weeks, when his first major brush with it ended in defeat. The company officer had seen it coming and passed command to him when they called for a second apparatus. Jace couldn't blame him.

"It's above you? Pull out, unit three."

"Can't tell if it's above yet. We may have time. It doesn't feel unsafe."

"Pull out," Jace repeated, firmer. "Do you copy?"

There was a pause before Pete answered. "I do. I don't think we need to be this cautious. We can save a lot more structure."

*They don't trust my judgement.*

Jace resisted the urge to stride up to the damn front door himself and drag Pete and Lou's asses out of the way.

But, no. He had to deal with this their way.

"Is the ceiling hot?"

"Lou says no, but the exterior wall is. If we pop it open and spray it now, we might keep it from getting that high."

Jace hated it. He wanted the guys out of there, but he recognized that Pete was right. It was his own damn demons. No reason to pull out of a safe working environment.

"Do it."

A minute later, with no answer, Jace started to get antsy. "Unit three?"

He held his breath until he got an answer. "Lots of smoke, not a lot of fire in here, Chief."

"Watch out. Anything could be hot, then." Under intense heat, especially with potential fuel droplets or fumes left, embers could reignite at any moment even in wet areas.

"Roger that."

One of the guys came up to Jace. "Sir. Chief Williams. The homeowner said to tell you he's got a tank of gas in the attic."

"Shit," Jace whispered. "The idiots."

"He's some kind of prepper."

Jace leaned heavily on the side of the engine and hit the mic. "Unit three. Guys, there's a tank of fuel in the attic. How big, did he say?" The firefighter shrugged. "We don't know how big. Probably a standard size."

"Copy that. We'll look out," Lou promised.

"I want you out the minute you see heat building up under the floor up there or jumping down from the wall, all right?"

"Yes, sir."

It was a nerve-racking few minutes. Jace kept an ear on the engineer, who controlled all the water his guys had access to, and his eyes on the house. There was another crew hosing down the outside of side D, too.

Then there were cops and rubberneckers to watch out for, and the distraught homeowners who didn't want to see them treat their house badly, even while saving it.

Jace was surprised how fast it was all over. The walls cooled off, the attic didn't catch, and they did several more walkthroughs to make damn sure the place was out before they left.

And, yeah, when push came to shove, Pete and Lou had agreed to leave the minute it became unsafe.

*It's not them not trusting me. It's me not trusting them to trust me.* The revelation was slow but absolute. Jace knew he came off as controlling sometimes, especially at a scene, but the instinct to jump in and rescue his guys suffused him. It was what had—almost always—kept everyone safe before now.

But it had to go both ways. He had to assume they knew what they needed.

Once he was back at the firehouse, post-shower and dressed in clean clothes, Jace realized why the realization had felt so big.

Charlie. He was assuming Charlie would need him to help with these big decisions—about his dad, his business, etc. But he had to ease off and let Charlie come to him.

Chasing him to the retirement home had been the right answer yesterday, but it wouldn't always be.

Which meant Jace had to admit it: he was afraid Charlie

would leave one day and not come back. The reason why was probably still lying in a hospital bed, having almost done exactly that.

*Not the time to dwell.* Jace killed that train of thought. The shift couldn't be over fast enough, but he was still working until Christmas morning.

On the bright side, he didn't have to spend it all at the house—he could go to his own home and rest, as long as he was ready to be on-call.

The morning's work had shown him exactly what he needed to do next, so after dinner, Jace spent his evening studying the inquiry's report.

Studying Hans's death.

Jace knew the answer to the exercise already, but doing it drilled it into his head. After reading the report and writing down everything that he could have done differently, he spent a while studying it.

If anything else had happened—if the variable wind conditions had shifted the other way, if the nearby fuel tank had exploded... if, if, if... those decisions would have been the wrong ones, and the ones he made were the right ones.

And all else aside, he was only human.

Jace was alone in bed that night, but not distraught to be so, like *that* night. He needed to face this alone. He put it off for an hour or so, but he finally crawled into bed, his work uniform folded neatly at the foot in case of a call, his phone plugged in.

Tonight, Jace's tears were his alone as he lay there in the dark, eyes closed but mind racing. The raw pain of the defining feature of humanity—needing to be loved despite his mistakes—made his chest ache.

But despite it, a long time after the tears slowed and his thoughts grew sluggish, Jace smiled.

*I'm ready to let someone try.*

## 26

## CHARLIE

He woke up alone again.

The first morning had been okay—Charlie was almost certain Jace's shifts started early in the morning, since Liam and Chris's did, too. It wasn't a surprise that Jace hadn't woken him if it had been early. Actually, it was kind of sweet.

Yesterday, he'd been able to distract himself by visiting his dad, then spending the day driving to a few cliffsides and beaches he hadn't used before to fly.

Today, though? It was Christmas Eve, and he'd heard barely a word from Jace.

At first, Charlie tried not to worry. Jace was no doubt swamped with administrative tasks. From the little Jace had said about his job, it sounded like it was more about scheduling, training, equipment requests, and those sorts of details than managing multiple-truck scenes.

Unit? Station? Engine? He'd have to ask. Like a little kid again, Charlie found himself curious what life was like for firefighters, but mostly for Jace.

"Oh, God."

It was Christmas Eve. That meant visiting his dad, and... he hadn't been doing well yesterday. He wasn't sure he could handle seeing him again today in that state.

*If that makes me a bad person, then it does. I can't look after him if I'm a wreck.*

Charlie just knew he shouldn't be alone tonight.

He could drive down and see Jemma, but she had her hands full with the kids and in-laws. And he was thirty, for Christ's sake. What kind of guy wound up crashing on his sister's couch because he couldn't handle being alone?

"Still don't even know if he's coming over," he mumbled to himself, looking around the apartment. But—what the hell, might as well.

Just in case.

He spent his morning cleaning, talking to himself, grumbling about all the housework he had to do... anything to keep his mind off being alone.

But the gnawing, itching urge deep in his stomach, and at the back of his head, never loosened its hold. His own frustration at his reactions was secondary, but nearly as strong.

*When did I let myself fall for him?*

Being vulnerable, needing one man's presence, didn't sit well with him. But neither did being alone. He was at the point where he had to decide, where he couldn't keep stringing Jace along if he couldn't do this, but *could* he do this? Could he be a good enough boyfriend?

Jace's fears, he understood and rejected. Jace was a good man who'd made a mistake in work, and maybe trusted too much in life.

But his own? Those were a lot harder to get a grip on.

Alone. He was alone, and it was his own fault.

Was he always going to be alone?

Fuck, even if he called a friend, confessed to these feelings and how damn hard it was to get them under control... it wasn't going to be enough.

He needed to talk to someone who loved him.

Maybe someone who still loved him, who'd always said he'd love him.

Halfway through dialing Justin's number, Charlie's breath caught in his throat. It was a stupid idea. He knew it, logically. But that damn number—all he had to type was 9834 and he wouldn't be alone today.

And Justin had always shown he loved him, even through not being able to control himself, hurting him.

"No. No," Charlie breathed out, then swore and tossed his phone on the couch. "Fuck it, Justin didn't deserve me." And he still didn't, even now.

If Charlie was going to seek out pain, he'd damn well do it himself.

He'd told himself years ago he wouldn't waste another drop of himself—cum, tears, or blood—on that man.

But this was about so much more.

It had been a long time since the mood seized him this completely, and he'd forgotten what it was like. Numb, yet afraid; lonely, yet antisocial. He couldn't reach out, couldn't admit weakness, but if someone spotted it in him, he'd accept their help.

Jace. When was Jace's shift over? He managed a quick text, his thumb shaking before he hit the Send button.

*Come straight over after work. Please.*

Why did his mind keep going back to being alone?

It took a while before he realized Jace had answered.

*I'm on call but I can be there in 10 minutes. Do you need me now?*

He typed out the answer, then pressed his phone to his forehead for a few long moments.

It wasn't life or death. He'd get through today on his own if he had to, as he had before. But it would sure as hell make his life easier right now, for these next few hours. It occurred to him that that was what Jace meant. Not whether he *needed* him to keep the blade out of his hand—and with a surge of relief, Charles realized that wasn't what he *really* wanted right now.

*Yes.*

*On my way.*

---

Jace's arms around him were like coming home. But they were at his house, so... it was like Jace brought home *with* him.

Charlie's cheeks burned. His lover handled his anxiety bravely and without complaint, but he couldn't handle a couple days alone?

He almost couldn't meet Jace's eyes, but he finally managed it as he pulled back from Jace's hug in the front hall. "Wanna sit down?"

"Of course."

Jace's work boots were heavy-duty. Probably the steel-toed, fire-resistant kind. Kind of sexy, when Charlie really thought about it.

"What's on your mind?"

There was the question he was dreading. It felt like he was a neglected potted herb—dried out but clinging to life. He'd just been drenched with the nourishment of human affection and contact, his flagging spirits slowly lifting.

"I saw Dad yesterday." The metaphor didn't come from nowhere. The drooping leaves of the potted plant in his kitchen made his cheeks flush with embarrassment, and he pulled away to water it before joining Jace on the couch. "He wasn't great. I can't do it today, but I'm feeling guilty, because..."

"Christmas," Jace murmured softly. "I get it. But you don't *owe* it to him. You've seen him other years, haven't you?"

"Every year for the last..." Charlie trailed off. "A while."

"And you have siblings."

"Two, but they can't... well, won't."

Jace frowned quietly, then slid his hand up Charlie's back to rub the back of his neck. "I see. Have you thought—"

His phone went off.

"Fuck. Damn it," Jace swore under his breath, pulling back from Charlie to check it. "Shit, it's work. I'm sorry. I—"

"No. No, you're at work," Charlie assured him.

Jace answered the phone, and from the terse conversation, it sounded bad. All Charlie heard from Jace's end was questions about where, how large it was, how long since the first apparatus had gotten there...

Charlie silently shadowed him to the door until Jace hung up.

Jace's eyes were torn as he took Charlie's hand. "Hon, if you're not going to be okay, you can ride along—"

"I'll be fine," Charlie shook his head. He wasn't going to risk distracting Jace when Jace was going to need all the focus he could get. And he even half-believed the words now.

Jace was his main concern.

"What about *you*?"

Jace pulled on his other boot, then straightened up, his face set in a determined expression. He was all business now. *That* was the kind of man Charlie would like to see striding through his doorway to save him. God, he was hot. *Not the time, Charlie.*

"I'll be fine," Jace echoed Charlie.

"Neither of us are *that* fine, huh?" Charlie added in an undertone, then smiled. "But Christmas Day...?"

"I'm off Christmas morning," Jace told him, pressing his lips against Charlie's forehead. "See you as soon as I can."

"Be safe."

Charlie almost regretted the words—what it must make Jace think of—but he had to say them, too. He had to have Jace home with him again, safe.

He pressed his fist to his mouth as he watched Jace's car peeling out of the driveway.

*I need him to be safe. Because I... need him.*

## 27

## JACE

The neighbors' house had already lit up by the time Jace got there. Three companies were on site, a fourth coming.

The last thing they needed if conditions shifted and the flames jumped the fence again was a whole-block fire. They already had a block and a half evacuated on Christmas Eve, kids and all.

Jace's breathing was tight, his thoughts rushing through the briefing. To make sure he got it all, he ran it through his head as he leaned on the engine, listening to the radio chatter.

One emergency company was already covering two other districts, so four was all they were getting. It should be enough, even for a two-structure complex fire like this.

*Break down the jobs. You know how.*

"Engine one, you're investigating, clearing the surroundings, right?"

"Affirmative, sir. It's contained well. Lots of distance between these places and the next houses."

Good. The first-due officer had passed command to the second, and Kevin had a good head on his shoulders.

That meant Liam and Chris were here—but so were a dozen other firefighters, all of whom were going to make it home safe to their families tonight.

The bad news: they had three civilians trapped upstairs in the second house. Everyone else had cleared out of nearby places; why couldn't they have?

"Unit three, you were on interior search. Do you copy?"

"Yes, sir. Cleared the downstairs floor. There's two minors, one adult upstairs."

They asked for another supply line and got it while Jace walked the perimeter with Kevin. "There's no other way out?"

"No," Kevin answered, grimacing. "It spread fast through the kitchen. Some cheap-build cabinets, it sounds like."

"Shit." Another matchbox house. Jace hated these places. The exterior operations officer met them, and the decision was made fast. They'd take side A—the front door. That meant a second company covering interior backup, now.

Jace watched them inside, his heart pounding.

He was a pro at *looking* calm, yeah, but feeling it? Fuck, no. Not on the inside. His palms sweated, his head spun, and he wanted to curl up and crawl under an engine.

It was the anxiety. He knew it. Didn't make it easier not to picture *that* day, even as he held the details about *this* one at the front of his mind.

*Lives are on the line. Again.*

The shadow of the day hung over them. Jace could feel it.

But while he'd been gone, they'd been training. His companies were working exactly as he'd told them to. One apparatus was on exterior defensive operations, making damn sure the dry Californian winter didn't invite disaster. The first house fire was almost under control, and they were working... well.

His brain clicked into gear.

"Ambulance," Jace murmured, then straightened up and

grabbed the radio to call for another ambulance. They'd need the first one to check over the civilians, and if his guys got into trouble, they'd need more EMTs.

He was going to use all the fucking resources he needed to stay ahead of this thing. Engine four was just arriving, so he radioed them to secure their own water supply.

The third and final civilian was leaving the second house, and moods were lifting.

Jace's heart rose, too.

Everyone was going home safe today. Nothing else mattered. His men trusted him, and he was not going to let them down. Not ever, *ever* again.

---

Fucking hazmat cleanup. It was the last thing anyone wanted to deal with so late on Christmas Eve that it was technically Christmas Day now, but it had to be done.

The investigator was a new guy who clearly didn't want to be there any more than Jace did, because he still wasn't on scene and Jace had been waiting an hour. Third time he'd had trouble with him now. He'd have to file a report or something... at least talk to his boss.

The staging area was largely broken down now—only one company left on scene, ambulances gone, a few tired-out guys and a food table with coffee. Thank God for coffee.

"Charlie, it's me." Jace leaned on the side of his car, glad he'd gotten voicemail and not woken Charlie up. "I won't be home for another couple hours. But the scene here's almost cleared. If you need anything, call me. Seriously. I'll be there as soon as I can."

Home, he'd said. Even though it wasn't his own house.

But home wasn't where his *house* was. It was where

Charlie was. The realization was as sudden and absolute as the moment he'd known he was going to marry Mike.

Jace rolled his head back and cracked his eyes open, staring at the false dawn. In the back of his head, he wondered how the parents around here would explain the fire to their kids. How they'd tell them Santa had landed safely on their rooftops or in their backyards, met the firefighters, maybe helped them out.

Did Charlie want kids? A house like this? To share *his* house?

He had so much to tell and ask... so much to share. So much to live for.

And today, Christmas of all days, seemed like the best time to show Charlie that once and for all.

He called back once more.

"Don't make plans today, baby. Unless those plans involve gliding. Then I want in on them. I want you to show me your favourite spots. Just don't record me, 'cause I'm gonna be scared shitless. Okay. Gone to finish work now. Bye."

## 28

## CHARLIE

The bed shifted next to him, and then a warm, solid arm slid over his shoulders.

Charlie smiled into the sleepy haze filtering through his mind. The smell of faint smoke clung to Jace, alerting some warning center in his brain, but it was all right. He didn't smell a bit like Justin.

He was *there*. Strong, solid, real. Whatever had happened at work, right now, he was safe.

Charlie pressed his cheek into Jace's hand, then slowly scooted closer to Jace until his back pressed into his lover.

The rough, soft voice in his ear murmured, "Merry Christmas."

"Love you, too."

Charlie slept.

What time was it? God, it had to be late in the morning, the angle the sun was at, and Jace was stirring beside him.

With how late—or early, rather—he'd been in, Charlie didn't want to move and wake him. He patted the bed by his pillow until he found his phone, but when he tapped on the button, the screen didn't wake.

It must have died yesterday. He hadn't charged it in a while. Thank God Jace hadn't needed to reach him.

Despite his best effort to keep still, Jace stirred again and stretched, turning slowly toward him and loosening his hold. He raised both arms to stretch, and Charlie cast an admiring look up at those biceps. Since Jace was up, he plugged in his phone to wake it up again.

"Good morning," Jace murmured.

"Merry Christmas." Then, Charlie's cheeks heated up. *Did I... last night... What did I say to him?* "You got in late."

"Very." Jace's voice had a catch of amusement in it, his eyes sparkling. He sat up, pushing the covers off. "You were out cold. Or almost."

Charlie groaned and covered his face. "I did say that, didn't I?"

"I know you meant you hate me. I won't hold it against you," Jace teased.

"Good." Fuck. Charlie could feel the blush creeping down his neck, to the tips of his ears. He rolled over, pressing his face into the pillow and moaning in protest. "Stop looking at me."

"I don't have to look at you to appreciate that sight." Through the comforter, Jace slapped Charlie's ass. "Mind if I grab a shower?"

"Of course. I showered last night anyway." Charlie resisted the urge to ask if Jace's shift had gone all right. He seemed to be in a fine mood, so nothing horrible had happened. There were tons of everyday fires that went well, weren't there?

He managed to sit up once Jace had stepped into the ensuite.

*He hasn't said he loves me back.*

But it was way too soon to expect that, Charlie knew it.

Charlie's thoughts were interrupted by a vibration next to the pillow. His phone went off with voicemails as it woke up, and, strangely, a text from his brother. He checked the text first.

*Merry XMAS :) Call me!*

That was strange for Brian. It wasn't like they didn't talk, but... it sounded like he needed something.

No point in putting it off. Charlie sighed and hit the call button.

"Hey, bro." Brian's voice was perky considering the hour. God, what time *was* it, anyway? Ten. That explained it.

"Hey. What's up?" Charlie answered.

"You just wake up? Lazy ass."

Charlie laughed. "Fuck you, it's Christmas. Merry Christmas."

Just like old times. Brian laughed richly. "You too. So, uh, I'm calling about Dad."

Charlie's good humor faded. He pushed the covers off himself and swung his feet out of bed. "Yeah?"

"I'm visiting him today. So don't worry about that. Go enjoy yourself."

It was the last thing Charlie had expected to hear, and his stunned silence probably spoke volumes. His mouth hung open for a few seconds.

Brian laughed. "Yeah. I can see you saying, *Wha'...?*"

"Who are you, and what have you done with Brian?" Charlie snorted.

Brian made a sound under his breath. "Mmm. You know. Things have changed."

"You all right?"

"I'm good. Fine, actually." Brian sounded thoughtful. "The band broke up, and I started thinking about things... Anyway, in the New Year, I'm going to school for something. A trade, I think."

Charlie's voice cracked. "*What?*"

"There it is. See?" Brian laughed. "Yeah. I know. But I've been thinking, I don't want to be thirty-something and practically broke, you know? Not gonna get the kind of girlfriend I want that way."

"Ohhh." Charlie's eyes narrowed. "Who do you have in mind?"

"The girl next door," Brian admitted. "But not just for *her*. For me, and you and Jemma, and Dad. It's time to grow up, I guess."

Charlie closed his eyes as he sat on the bed, then rubbed his face. "I'm proud of you, man."

"Thanks. So you're gonna take the day off? You see him, what, once a week?"

"If I'm busy, yeah. I try to go every other day, keep him company." Charlie didn't say it, but he didn't have to—he was trying to make up for all three of them.

"Wow. Well, you know, we can... share that. Depending on my school or job. We'll figure it out."

Charlie shook his head. "Love makes a guy do crazy things, doesn't it?"

Brian paused before he answered. "Huh. And *that* sounds like *you* have something to tell me."

*Not until I figure things out with him.* "Maybe. We should meet up, grab a beer."

"Come over next week," Brian told him. "We can catch up."

Charlie's face broke into a grin. He couldn't remember the last time his brother had invited him over. "Yeah. I'd like that."

"Okay. Take care. I gotta call Jemma now, too. Merry Christmas," Brian wished him.

Charlie was dressed by the time Jace came back to the bedroom, still smiling to himself.

"So, where are we going today?"

Charlie blinked at Jace, who blinked back. After a moment, Jace added, "Got my voicemail last night?"

"Oh! No. My phone died, and then my brother called." Charlie held up a finger and checked his voicemail.

Jace looked amused, propping a hand on his hip. Also sexy, especially with his towel only loosely knotted near his hipbone. "I can just tell you what I said."

"Shhh." Charlie listened to Jace's messages.

The offer to call him if he needed anything at all didn't go over Charlie's head. Jace had been right to be worried, but Charlie had managed on his own. Charlie offered a grateful smile and looked down again, waiting for the second.

"...Hang-gliding?" Charlie didn't want to be *too* delighted in case he'd changed his mind. Jace, in the *air*?

Jace sighed and shook his head as he grabbed his bag from the door. Apparently he'd picked up a change of clothes some-where—home, before coming here? "God knows what I was thinking."

"Oh my God, hon. You don't *have* to," Charlie insisted, but he was already beaming.

Jace grinned back at him, zipping up his jeans. Shame to make that gorgeous cock disappear. "When you're looking at me like that? I do now."

"So this gaze works? I'll keep that in mind for later." Charlie winked.

His heart was already light. He'd start Jace somewhere nice and easy. There wouldn't be a lot of people out on his favorite cliffs on Christmas Day. That would make for a nice easy tandem foot launch.

"A quick breakfast and then we'll go?" Jace smiled. "And Chinese takeout for dinner?"

Charlie sauntered toward the kitchen, letting his hips sway. "Delivery."

"*Ohh*. Agreed."

Charlie hummed and poured cereal for them both, then grabbed glasses. Before he could grab the milk and juice, Jace set them down beside him, then wrapped his arms wrapped around Charlie's waist.

Charlie leaned back into that solid chest, half-smiling and not even bothering to try to open the containers yet. He gently rested his hands on Jace's, closing his eyes.

"Me, too. Against the odds," Jace murmured into his ear.

Charlie's breath caught in his throat and his hand went still against Jace's. There was only thing he could be referencing. Did he mean...?

"Cool," he laughed under his breath, suddenly flustered. Oh, God. He couldn't think of anything better than *that* to say? That was terrible.

Jace laughed. "Hurry up, before I lose my nerve."

*And say I love him again, or...? Oh! No!* Of course Jace meant the hang-gliding. Charlie told himself off for jumping to conclusions as he poured their juice and milk for their cereal, then brought the bowls to the table.

It was hard to eat breakfast while smiling this hard.

---

"That was easy! That was *great*. And easy. Gentle! I can't believe we were that high up...!"

All the way back to Jace's house, he hadn't stopped talking his ear off. If Charlie's cheeks had hurt earlier from smiling, they were *aching* now from grinning.

Watching a first-timer was always fun, but especially Jace. He'd been stoic but clearly nervous before takeoff, and then… then, he'd seen the thrill.

They'd taken three flights together, each one progressively longer as Jace lost his nerves and built confidence.

"You wanna go again, is what you're telling me," Charlie teased. He locked up the car and swaggered around to the other side.

He *loved* showing off his passion, and Jace had just signed himself up to hear all about it.

"I wouldn't hate you if you took me again," Jace supplied with a grin. "How's that?"

"Damn. You're falling down on our mutual dislike. But that's acceptable." Charlie took his hand, following him inside. "God, your house is pretty."

"Empty, though."

Charlie didn't think so—it was a good use of space, and any empty places could easily be filled with pieces…

Oh. He wasn't talking about physically.

Charlie cast a quick look up at Jace. "Don't be shy about it."

"Fine." Jace cleared his throat, then smiled. "I'm just saying… if money's a concern with your new bills and all… you rent, don't you?"

"Yeah." *Holy crap, he's going there.* Charlie tried not to bounce with excitement like he was seeing his first grownup apartment. "So you're inviting me to move in, and we haven't even asked each other to be boyfriends yet."

He tried to project it with his thoughts. *Yes. Yes, I'm ready.* But he didn't have to worry.

Jace scoffed and rolled his eyes. "Fine, I *guess*." He slid his arm around Charlie's waist and yanked him in.

Charlie laughed at the sudden tug, stumbling into Jace's

chest and bracing himself against it. "Asshole." For that, he pinched Jace's nipple.

"Ow! Jerk. Be my boyfriend?"

"I *guess*," Charlie imitated Jace, rolling his head back. "If I *have* to be, I could put up with you. Both as my boyfriend, and... living here."

"As long as the sex is good?"

Charlie hummed and nodded slowly, trying not to grin. "I think you should give me a demonstration. Just to be sure."

"A demo? It may take me a while to find a guy to demonstrate with me—" Jace started, but Charlie cut him off by pinching his other nipple. "*Ow*! Will you stop that? Jesus."

"Make me," Charlie challenged, a grin spreading across his face. Just as Jace reached for his shoulder to haul him close, Charlie jerked away, wiggling out of his hold and sprinting for the stairs. "If you can."

For a few seconds, he wondered: why wasn't Jace chasing?

He realized a few steps up that Jace had purposely given him a lead, because he was so damn sure he'd catch up.

*That* was hot.

Jace crossed the living room, climbing the stairs in solid, long-legged strides, his eyes focused on Charlie.

Who was thinking about the way that made his cock stir to life, and wasn't looking where he was going, and stumbled against the steps. The adrenaline rushed as he gasped, and then—

Jace's hands were there on his sides, pulling him to his feet and up, over his shoulder.

The slap he gave Charlie's ass was a lot harder than the first time they'd done this. It *stung*, but holy *fuck*, did it burn so nicely. It sent electric shivers of need reverberating through his body, head to toe, fingers to the hard-on that was pressing into Jace's shoulder again.

"Oh my God," he moaned.

Jace's voice was a deep rumble from behind and above him, which reminded him—he had an *awesome* view of his ass.

"That all right?"

Charlie couldn't think of words except, "Fuck, yeah, it is."

"Hmm." Jace's voice was teasing. They were up the stairs and in the bedroom now.

Charlie's world shifted as he found himself flung through the air just the short distance, falling hard on the mattress while Jace scrambled over him. He fought his t-shirt off as Jace did the same, and both of them went for each other's jeans zippers and buttons.

Fuck, he needed this.

He *wanted* this.

Not just the sex... the man.

"I want you. Baby, I—I meant it last night." The words fell out of his lips before he even thought twice about them.

Jace's hand cupped his bulge, making it really damn hard to focus on the way his lips moved. Wait, that wasn't the important part. The words.

"I love you, too."

Relief surged through Charlie, who closed his eyes for a moment, then managed a giddy little smile as he met Jace's eyes again. *I was waiting for that.*

"I think... from the moment we met." His eyes were dark, intense, stunning Charlie into silence. "I wasn't ready to admit it, but there was something."

"Yeah," Charlie whispered. He knew exactly what Jace meant. That crackle between them, the way they couldn't tear their attention off each other... it was a lot easier to interpret as dislike than love.

But the reward of love was so much higher.

Charlie had come out ahead, with *this* man above him,

currently slipping his hand into his underwear to palm his hard shaft. "Oh, fuck," Charlie whimpered, pushing hard into Jace's hand and trying to rub. "Yes. Yes, please, please..."

"We have all day," Jace chuckled deeply.

"You use that as an excuse to tease me or blue-ball me and I'll be fucking pissed," Charlie informed him.

"Damn. There goes that plan. I was thinking I'd make you come until you can't remember your own name."

Suddenly, Charlie couldn't think straight past the desire that surged through him. He wanted Jace in him, on him, around him... licking, sucking, fucking, touching, pinching, *anything*.

"Need you," he managed, rolling his head back against the pillow and grabbing Jace's shoulders. "Baby."

Jace's lips pressed against his chest, then the side of his neck. "What do you want?"

"In me, first. Fuck me."

"Not starting slowly?" Jace's voice dripped with meaning. In those few syllables, Charlie got a flash of what he might mean: Jace's hands running slowly down his body, or his mouth on his nipples, or his palm coming down hard on his throbbing ass until his dick screamed for attention...

God, as tempting as it was, it wasn't what he wanted first. "No. In me," he repeated.

Jace's hand cupped his cheek as he nestled between his thighs, pushing his legs up against his chest. "I've got you," he promised in a whisper, then pressed their lips together.

Kissing Jace was divine. When Charlie kissed him, nothing else mattered, or even existed. It was just their bodies, their souls, their hearts. Their broken hearts, each meticulously stitched together, but no smaller for the confinement they'd been placed under.

Slick fingers pressing into him were nice—by God, were

they ever—but not what Charlie needed. He moaned in protest, but Jace ignored him, swallowing his moans and kissing them right back at him.

Jace took his time sliding his fingers in and out. He went slowly at first, and then in quick rhythm that seemed to fall in time with Charlie's harsh breathing. He rubbed back and forth across that sensitive spot deep inside until the nerves pricked to life.

God, yes. If he'd needed him before, it was a raw, physical level where Charlie needed Jace now.

"Skip the condom. I haven't gone with anyone since you," Charlie breathed out. Even that was fucking weird, but one more thing he could get used to.

Jace's voice rumbled by his ear as he kissed a slow line toward it, making Charlie shiver and flinch with need. "Me neither. You sure?"

"You better get that cock in me before I come on the spot, but yeah."

Jace laughed softly, and then the fingers were gone and Charlie was empty. Fucking empty, but not alone.

No, Jace was there with him, his body pressing against Charlie's, keeping him grounded and *there*, yet flying.

When Jace's tip pressed against him, Charlie caught his breath and then grunted. His breathing cut the noise out.

"Don't go quiet on me now," Jace teased.

"What?"

Jace moaned, his voice rough and his eyes... God, the way he watched Charlie, like he wanted to drink him up. "You don't even know half the sounds you make, do you? Fucking hot."

Charlie grabbed Jace's hips and pulled him in, pushing against him as much as he could with his knees by his chest. "*Now.*"

Jace filled him, inch by inch. It was so tight it was almost painful, but the burn of his cock head sliding across his prostate was too good to turn down.

"Oh, fuck," Charlie whimpered. "Nnnh, baby!"

Jace whispered against his ear, "I love being around you, and I *love* being in you." His lips trailed down Charlie's neck, then up his throat as Charlie rolled his head back. "I hope you weren't looking for slow and sweet."

When he could catch his breath, Charlie snorted derisively. "Slow and sweet."

"That's not us, is it?" Jace laughed richly.

"Not from the start." Nothing about either of them, let alone the two of them together, was slow nor sweet... but it was perfect for them. Well, Jace was a lot sweeter than he'd let on, but Charlie let that one go.

Charlie was ready for more than these shallow, slow thrusts. He growled under his breath, his nails digging into Jace's back.

That always worked. Jace flinched, then gasped and dove in for a harder kiss, their lips sliding hot and wet against one another's as he started to thrust hard, fast, *deep* inside Charlie.

Charlie's body was on fire with need. Every rub of their bare skin on skin, every tingle of Jace's lips sucking on his own, every electric tingle of his prostate and answering throb of his dick...

Oh, his body was tight already, his stomach sucked in so tight he could hardly breathe. His arms locked around Jace's back, his head rolling back as he finally took the time and space he needed to breathe. Just for a second.

Just to try to hold out a minute longer, to draw out this intimacy between them as long as he possibly could...

"Jace...!" Charlie gritted out. He couldn't help it. His toes curled, his eyes squeezed shut, he slid his arm between their bodies to jerk himself off.

The mattress creaked as Jace drove into him, his nails biting into Charlie's hip to hold him in place. His breathing was ragged, but he managed Charlie's name in a rough, deep voice.

A few sharp tugs along his shaft, already slick with how fucking close he was, and Charlie came undone. "Yes!"

His body clenched and shivered in waves of passion, squeezing around Jace as Jace gasped his name in his ear and came, too, hard.

Sweaty and ecstatic, locked in each other's arms and sticky with passion, they rode out the waves of pleasure for a minute with jerky thrusts and throaty moans.

When Charlie could finally breathe, he let his arms fall away from Jace and pushed his feet down the bed, sprawling against it to gasp. "Jesus."

"No, it's Jace."

Charlie groaned. "That's not even funny," he complained, but he couldn't stop a breathless laugh picking up at the end of his sentence.

Jace let that stand for itself and grinned, all smarmy now.

"Shut up," Charlie snorted, pulling Jace onto him and wrestling until he was on top.

"Oh, this is how you want round two to go?"

Charlie was glowing despite himself. He folded his arms and sat up, enjoying the view. "Yep. We'll start here and see what happens."

"Mmhmm." Jace laced his fingers behind his head, his eyes half-closed as he gazed up at Charlie.

Charlie couldn't stop himself leaning down again, pressing his lips against Jace's. "I fucking love you. So there."

Air warmed his lips from Jace's laugh, and then Jace kissed him gently in return. "I love you too, so deal with it."

"Fine. I suppose."

Charlie rolled off Jace and nestled into his side after a

moment. The strong arm pulling him into his chest made it all worth it.

*They say you know when you've found the one. They don't say you'll know the first moment you meet, and you'll get scared, and you'll do everything you can to avoid it.*

Charlie gave one more delirious grin, pressing his lips into Jace's shoulder and closing his eyes.

*But it was worth it. For him.*

"How long 'til midnight?"

"Three minutes."

"Oooh." Charlie looped his arm around Jace's. "Better not lose track of you, then."

It wasn't like they'd get separated and go very far. This New Year's Eve party was small—along with the two of them, it was just Liam, Dylan, Chris, and Ash.

Some other friends had stopped by to visit earlier, but now it was just them. Three couples. Charlie was almost embarrassed at how happy that made him.

"Separate? You two?" Dylan snorted with laughter. "As if."

"Shut up," Charlie rolled his eyes, but it was true. He'd been squished into the corner of the sofa, half-on Jace's lap, most of the evening. "He won't keep his hands off me, that's all."

Jace raised his brow and looked down at their locked arms.

"That's beside the point." Everyone laughed, and Charlie's cheeks flushed. "It's a good thing he's pretty."

Jace hummed. "I'll take that."

"You'd better," Charlie threatened. "You're running up against your compliment limit for the night."

"When did you compliment me before?" Jace laughed.

Oh. Right. "Fine. You're allowed one more." Charlie blushed and sipped his beer again.

He'd been talking with Ash in the kitchen when he'd mentioned how hard Jace had worked with him to help him pack and move things, even in this crazy week between Christmas and New Year's.

It was a fast move, neither of them denied that. At Jace's family's post-Christmas get-together, when he'd met them, they'd all said as much in a tone that frankly annoyed Charlie.

What did they know? It felt right.

Apart from work and moving, they'd spent the week barely out of Jace's—now *their*—bed. They cooked together, hung out together in the evenings, brought each other out to hang out with their friends.

Jace had missed this routine, Charlie could tell. And Charlie had been living alone for a whole lot longer, and then before, sharing space with Justin... not even close to comparable.

It was like he'd been holding his breath for a very long time, stubbornly refusing to open his eyes.

And now he was here, his chest about to burst with warmth and affection for all the guys here, but most of all, Jace.

Dylan was sitting on Liam's lap, his arm around his neck, cheek on his shoulder. He chattered about the TV special and how he wanted to go to New York City, and Liam nodded along.

Ash and Chris had been glowing nonstop since the engagement day. No wonder, with the whirlwind they'd gone through, but Charlie had never seen Ash look happier. Except, perhaps, when he'd been standing at the altar for the wedding.

All four husbands were happy, and that made Charlie happy. Even though they were still getting to know every bit of each other, so were the two of them.

Jace couldn't fix Charlie, or vice versa. They were both wounded, and still healing. But they were better with each other, and they worked harder on their habits and thoughts for each other.

Charlie was always going to deal with the coping mechanisms he'd learned early, he knew already. It would always be in the back of his mind at a particularly stressful moment.

But all he had to do was keep choosing to live. Even if that meant reminding himself now and then that he was alive by flinging himself off a cliff. He'd always keep a hang-glider attached to him, at least.

And Jace's anxiety? He'd had a few attacks in the last week, but he handled them on his own, and he didn't look half-dead with exhaustion afterward. He slept better, ate better, smiled more.

"Hey, you." Jace was nudging him, a smile on his face as he pointed at the TV. "Thirty seconds. Don't miss the ball dropping."

"Oh!" Charlie jolted to wakefulness again and shook his head. "I like balls dropping. Thanks for pointing that out. Can we drop more later?"

Jace still got embarrassed with PDA sometimes, but he grinned back at him. "Cheeky monkey."

"I know. Good thing you love me." Charlie pecked Jace's lips.

Jace kissed him back. The other guys laughed, counting down from ten, but he didn't stop.

Charlie chuckled against Jace's lips and shook his head, but he sucked Jace's lip between his own and leaned in anyway. *Ridiculous man.*

Jace's hands ran up his hips to his sides, holding him there, so Charlie looped both arms around Jace's neck and tilted his head, pressing against him as hard as he could.

Their lips slid together, warm and wet and perfect—

"Three," Charlie teased, pecking and pulling back. "Two..." He did it again.

Jace's eyes sparkled. He joined in for, "One...", and then...

Then, they kissed like the world was ending. Or maybe like their lives were beginning. Not lives... their *life*, together, forever.

# AFTERWORD

Dear reader,

Thank you for reading *Aftermath*. This was the final book in the After series, easily one of my hardest series to write. It brings me great relief to give happily-ever-after endings to these guys.

I hope the happily-ever-after endings for all of the guys in this series have made up for the hard journeys to get there! Take care of yourself, and please seek support if you need to.

Thank you to my Facebook group, Ed's Petals, for embracing and uplifting this series, along with all my other books. This was such a hard series to write! If it touches you, please consider leaving a review so others can find it, too.

Make sure you sign up for my newsletter to hear about: exclusive free short stories and sales; new releases in ebook, audio, and print; preorder alerts; sneak peeks at upcoming books; event appearances; and other exciting news as it happens!

I also have a reader group on Facebook if you want to chat about your favorite parts of *Aftermath*, see cute bee photos and good news stories, and keep on top of my upcoming releases with a whole bunch of lovely readers: https://www.facebook.com/groups/edavies

Last but not least: always be you!

~Ed

## HARD HART

### I felt all wrong until I met you.

Jesse Stone is rebuilding his life. He's ditched his no-good ex, sworn off men, moved to a new town with his four best friends, and started the pottery business of his dreams. And then he slept with his hunky new neighbor. Oops. Jesse needs to focus on work, but all he can think about is getting Finn between his hands like a perfectly-shaped work of clay.

Trouble just blew into town, and his name is Jesse. Finn Hart knows that pursuing Jesse will ignite old family tensions, but he can't stay away. The construction foreman has never built a lasting relationship. He's too busy keeping the peace in a town that was founded by one Hart, but is slowly being strangled by another— Finn's grandfather.

Finn and Jesse are on the same page: they want to save Hart's Bay, and it starts by bringing tourists in with Jesse's new art gallery. But their hearts are bruised, and taking a chance comes with a price. Not everyone in Hart's Bay wants change. For a few narrow minds, nothing good should come to Finn's branch of the Harts, and that includes love.

Can love wash away twenty years of bad blood and bring a new dawn for Jesse, Finn, and all of Hart's Bay?

*Hard Hart is the first book in the new Hart's Bay series about a small town full of nosy but well-meaning neighbors and brotherly banter. It can be read on its own, and promises a happily-ever-after ending and plenty of smiles and steam along the way. If that cove could talk... oh boy, has it ever seen things.*

# ABOUT THE AUTHOR

E. Davies grew up moving constantly, which taught him what people have in common, the ways relationships are formed, and the dangers of "miscellaneous" boxes. As a young gay author, Ed prefers to tell feel-good stories that are brimming with hope.

He writes full-time, goes on long nature walks, tries to fill his passport, drinks piña coladas on the beach, flees from cute guys, coos over fuzzy animals (especially bees), and is liable to tilt his head and click his tongue if you don't use your turn signal.

 facebook.com/edaviesbooks

twitter.com/edaviesauthor

 instagram.com/thisboyisstrange

bookbub.com/authors/e-davies

**Brooklyn Boys:**

Electric Sunshine

Live Wire

Boiling Point

**F-Word:**

Flaunt

Freak

Faux

Forever

**After:**

Afterburn

Afterglow

Aftermath

**Men of Hidden Creek:**

Shelter

Adore

Miracle

Redemption

**Coauthored with Zach Jenkins:**

Sugar Topped

Just a Summer Deal

**Audiobooks:**

The list is growing rapidly! You can see all my books available in audio here: www.edaviesbooks.com/audiobooks